THEY ALL [illegible]

No one wh[illegible] l live if he were co[illegible] of the three men [illegible] Remo. But there w[illegible]

"Well, yo[illegible] Your abilities far [illegible]

"So?" said [illegible]

"So there is only one man on earth equipped to kill you now."

"No," said Remo.

He couldn't believe it. He wouldn't believe it. He had to find out.

"Little father. They tell me you are going to kill me," Remo said.

Chiun, Master of Sinanju, the man who taught Remo that a bullet can be dodged and a leap off the Statue of Liberty is no different than any other first step, looked closely at him. "Don't call me little father," he said.

WARREN MURPHY & RICHARD SAPIR

REMO
UNARMED AND DANGEROUS

Based on the original screenplay by
Christopher Wood

Futura

A Futura Book

First published by New American Library, New York

First published in Great Britain in 1986 by
Futura Publications, a Division of
Macdonald & Co (Publishers) Ltd
London & Sydney

All characters in this publication are fictitious and any resemblance to real persons, living or dead, is purely coincidental.

ISBN 0 7088 3137 0

Reproduced, printed and bound in Great Britain by
Hazell Watson & Viney Limited,
Member of the BPCC Group,
Aylesbury, Bucks

Futura Publications
A Division of
Macdonald & Co (Publishers) Ltd
Maxwell House
74 Worship Street
London EC2A 2EN
A BPCC plc Company

For Larry Spiegel,
who made it happen

1

Sam Makin was dead a day and a half before someone finally showed him his obituary. He couldn't read past the headline by himself because his eyes wouldn't focus. His head felt like it had been engraved with a tin can, and there were bandages covering most of his face.

He tried to swallow but his crack-dry tongue had first priority on any moisture his mouth could generate.

"It was a grand funeral," came the voice. "The mayor was there. Your precinct captain was there. Your lieutenant was there. Your desk sergeant was there. And of course, I was there. I had to be. I had to make sure you didn't have any really close friends."

The voice was almost joyful. So was the smooth black face just within Makin's peripheral vision. The man wore an expensive hat and well-tailored jacket. Sam tried to breathe. His ribs hurt. The man talked about funerals. Somehow Sam Makin's funeral had been this man's problem.

"You never know who shows up at a funeral.

It's like a poultice for acquaintances of life. Do you know what a poultice is?"

Sam Makin groaned.

"It's a packet of herbs that draws out the poisons from wounds. We didn't know who, or what, would be drawn out by your funeral. We might have found out you had a mother or a father. You might have even had a friend who cared about you. There could have been complications."

Sam Makin groaned again.

"Were you hoping, laddie, that you had a mother who would remember you? Were you hoping that?"

Sam took in the expensive cashmere of the man's jacket. The fingernails buffed to a high gloss. The man seated himself on one side of the thin foam mattress, talking on with that same cheerful malevolence.

"Not even a girlfriend showed up, although you had a lot of those in your day. Too many. Never cheated on one of them either, loyal man that you were. It was one woman at a time, for a week, a month. You were even engaged three times in one year. And not one of them came to your graveside; not a single rose was sent. Nothing. You want to see all your friends, your relatives? Do you think I am lying to you?"

Sam Makin tried to move his head. He did not know if it was the pain that held it on the pillow, or a heavy weight. He could tell the sheets on the bed he was lying in were white. The walls of the room were white. The bed had white bars at the foot, with a clipboard attached. And he smelled ether. Or did he taste it? There were bandages on his head. He was in a hospital.

The well-dressed black man busied himself with something at the foot of the bed. A short metal tripod and a small screen. Why was he saying these cruel things? What was he doing?

"Can you focus yet? They tell me you might have a wee bit of difficulty in focusing at first."

Sam Makin tried to speak. The word came out with sharp pains in the back of his throat. His voice sounded odd, like a stranger's voice. The word he said was:

"Who?"

But the stranger didn't let him finish the sentence. The screen at the foot of the bed lit up. There was a graveside. A coffin rested between two pulley cords. A priest read a eulogy for Sam. It was very brief. It talked about duty. The priest didn't even say he was a good man. He only talked about duty. Sam could see the pictures of the mourners. One mayor. One precinct captain. One desk sergeant. Six men from his Brooklyn precinct, obviously recruited as pallbearers. And when the camera pulled away Sam could see that very big graveyard and the handful of living people who had come there for him.

The mayor spoke exactly one sentence: "Patrolman Sam Makin gave his life so that the people of Brooklyn might live in a safer city." There wasn't even a newspaper photographer. Sam had been the seventh patrolman killed that year. No story in that. Then the pictures on the screen ran through close-ups of the few people gathered at the graveside. Close-up of a face, then a pause. On to the next subject, and a pause. Suddenly Sam realized, realized too late, that the man sitting on his bed was controlling the film, manipulating the lapses between images. The man was studying something on his lap, an electronic device, and it was connected to Sam himself. Wires ran from Sam's wrists to a monitor.

The man was reading Sam's reactions to the faces on the screen.

"Nope, not a friend there, laddie. No momma. No poppa. Not a friend in the world." The man was actually happy.

"Who," said Sam Makin, "are you?"

He had finished his question.

"Me?" said the man cheerfully rolling up the wires to the monitor. "I'm the man who killed you." On the screen at his feet, the picture suddenly speeded up, apparently released from the controls, and there, center screen, was the shiny wood coffin, lowering into the grave, and someone saying, "Good-bye, Sam Makin."

Even the priest didn't say anything more about him. As everyone left, the camera sound picked up talk of basketball and the New York Knicks, retirement allowances and how the New York City police force had to have a new summer uniform.

"Like today really made me think," came the voice of Sam's old desk sergeant. "We're all out here wearing winter uniforms and it's a warm day. But the summer uniforms aren't that much better. You know. I was thinking that, watching the priest. Even in a surplice, a priest is better dressed for the weather than we are."

And then the screen went blank, and Sam Makin remembered how he had died. He had heard that sergeant's voice at the end, and at the beginning. The sergeant had been working radio control. Patrolman Makin had been doing a solo cruise on the waterfront. He remembered how beautiful New York City looked across the East River. He remembered watching the barge loaded with happy dancers being pulled out for an evening under the Brooklyn Bridge. He remembered listening to the end of a tight Knicks game on his own little transistor, and taking a short break with a cup of coffee. And Sam Makin remembered the sergeant's voice.

"Twenty-one sixteen," the sergeant's voice crackled over the radio. It was Sam's patrol car he was calling. The short break was over. Sam turned off the game, stuffed his Styrofoam coffee cup down a model of Miss Piggy he kept just under the dashboard, somewhat against regulations. This was an NYPD police car, and according to regulations there "shall be no foreign accoutrements not directly in support of police duties." But he had kept Miss Piggy. As he had told so many people, she seemed to be the one woman who stayed by him.

"Twenty-one sixteen," said Sam.

"You got another couple hours on the graveyard shift," came the sergeant's voice.

"Great," said Sam. He had been counting on a pizza with extra cheese, and a glass of beer. The closer his shift came to an end, the more he could taste the sharp smooth cheese and the rich foamy beer. The respite that had been fifteen minutes away had now become a two-hour-and-fifteen-minute stretch.

"Look at it this way. You can hear the rest of the Knicks on city time."

Sam smiled. The sergeant knew him. Actually the two hours didn't matter. It had been one of those weeks. Hell, it had been one of those months. Sam Makin would remember in the hospital that it had been one of those months. It had started with the reaction time drills. Apparently some idiot in Washington had decreed that for cities to get certain matching funds for their police departments, every patrolman under a certain age had to take a battery of reflex tests.

Sam didn't know he had scored well until he was rewarded, with another test. And this was even crazier. It was a psychological evaluation. Sam recalled question number five as if the printed form were still before him.

"How do you imagine your mother and father would look if you saw them?"

It didn't take a genius to figure out that everyone in the examination room was an orphan. Then there were other questions. Finally some he just refused to answer.

He had brought the test up to the proctor. An honest woman from Toledo, Ohio.

"You can take this, lady, and do you-know-what. You can have the job. I am not answering these questions. There are some things I just will not do."

"Very good," she said and smiled.

At the time, three weeks before the night he spent waiting near the East River, the night he would die, Sam had been dating a psychology major at City College. Like so many before her, Sam had thought she could have been the one, the right woman for him.

She recognized some of the questions he repeated for her.

"That's the standard test for the compulsive-obsessive, authority-oriented, social-avenger types."

"What are you talking about?"

"It's a kind of a patriot."

"What do you mean some kind of a patriot?" Sam asked, hoping Sheila wouldn't turn out like all the others. Sheila Winsted had seemed so reasonable up until this point. Reasonable, in addition to a dynamite smile and a body that could turn heads a hundred yards away.

"There is a type that can function alone driven by a compulsion. And that compulsion is socially oriented. They feel that things are not right in the world, and that they should be made right. They have a very strong sense of justice."

"That's good," said Sam. "That's a good thing to have. Why are you describing it like some sort of insanity?"

"Well, it is a form of deviant behavior. All heroism is."

"That's the trouble with schools today. That's the trouble with America. When you start calling the patriots sick, then the country is sick."

"Sam, were there some questions on that test you refused to answer?"

"You're damned right."

"Then they got you. Those are the key questions that nail them every time. Sometimes these patriots can hide behind the answers they give, but they can't hide behind the questions they won't answer."

"Those questions were obscene. They had no right to get answers to them."

"Sam," said Sheila Winsted with the dazzling smile. "You are one."

"And you're a ball buster," said Sam.

"Like all the rest of them?" asked Sheila.

"Yeah. Like all the rest of them."

"Often your kind has an inability to establish a lasting contact with anyone, although you do have a great need for love."

"Hey, Sheila," said Sam, grabbing her shoulders. "Look at me. I am a human being. I am a person. I'm not a type."

"Don't take it personally," said Sheila.

"You're calling me a nut, and I am not supposed to take it personally? You're crazy, Sheila."

And that of course had ended the affair with Sheila Winsted, leaving Sam Makin with the only one who was always there for him—Miss Piggy. Miss Piggy was with him that night. The last night.

The desk sergeant had just checked in one more time, when Sam saw a thin black youngster zipping sneaker-fast across the front of his squad car. Two white men ran after him. When the youngster careened toward a warehouse pier the whites stayed right on his tail.

Sam, headlights off on the squad car, slowly eased it out of position onto the street, following the running men. The two whites caught up with the black man just at the warehouse wall. Sam drove the squad car right up behind them, and drawing his 38-caliber special, slammed on the brakes and was out of the car in an instant.

"Freeze," he said. He had the convincer right in his hands, sighted on all three of them. He could drop them all in less than a second. He was a top marksman at the range.

The trio got the message. Sam Makin had that kind of a voice. People knew he would shoot. Their hands went up above their heads.

"Over to the car," said Makin. "Move it. Hands on the car. That's it." The two white men leaned against the car as though they had done this before.

"Spread 'em," said Makin. The young black man was not that young, close up. He looked all right, just a bit groggy. Makin turned his back on him. He would help him later.

But he didn't have a chance to help. He knew he didn't have a chance to help when the bat came cracking across the side of his head. Trying to swing it again was the black man he had been trying to save. He was panting out some kind of instruction to the whites. Sam felt the warm blood on the side of his face, the dullness that would precede great pain, the ringing in his head. His legs wanted to give out, but there was something in him that didn't let him fall. He looked for his gun. It was on the wharf, sickeningly spinning away from him as the bat came back at his head. He felt his own hands on the bat, catching the force, catching the numbing hurt in a myriad of delicate bones and tissue, but the hands held. Screaming out in pain, he yanked the bat free and rammed it back, handle forward, into the giving groin of the black, who gasped like a broken water bag and fell useless to the wharf.

Makin wasn't thinking. He was swinging. He felt the reassuring crunch of a jaw under his elbow. One of the white hoods had a hammerlock on his head and was trying to bring him down. But Sam smashed his own head into the man's nose, butting hard, feeling nothing. And then there was that reassuring crack of a face under his fist, and he kept sending it back into the teeth, into the jaw, hitting until the face was falling from him.

And then there was one. But that one had a switchblade. Sam could run for his car and get help. He could dive for his gun and probably get the knife in his back. He could also back away. The man wasn't coming after him.

Sam decided to make him move—take a run at him. On the first step, the hoodlum turned to flee. But Sam got him in three good strides, kicking the feet out from under him, sending the hoodlum crashing into stacked garbage cans.

It was over. Sam casually went over to the man, grabbed his belt buckle and with one hand hoisted him up, and then head forward dumped him into an open can.

"Don't eat too much," said Sam. He retrieved his gun, handcuffed the one hood who seemed most able to run. It was the black man.

"What was that about?" asked Sam. "You working with them? Why were you running if you tried to help them?"

The black man didn't answer. Sam lifted him in the air by his armpits and informed him of his rights. He informed him he had a right to remain silent. But he also informed him that he did not have a right to be held aloft over the wharf planking. And on that Sam dropped him. Then lifted him. And informed him of these rights again.

This invariably changed a criminal's mind about talking. In fact, this simple technique had always worked so well that despite five citations for bravery, Sam Makin was still a patrolman. A patrolman with four charges for police brutality. He had been warned a good half dozen times just to do his job.

"We are policemen, Makin. This isn't good guys versus bad guys. Everyone is equal under the law. And whether you like it or not, people are innocent until proven guilty."

"And what if someone has a knife in the back of a little old lady?"

"You arrest him, and let the judge decree punishment."

He had heard that several times. And it struck him as odd on that wharf that night, with New York City twinkling massive across the dark East River, that the very same questions Sam had asked his sergeant had appeared on that funny test, the one whose last questions he refused to answer. It also seemed strange that after three drops onto the wharf planking the hoodlum was still not talking.

In a curious way, Sam Makin admired the man for not talking. At least he had guts. Sam admired him one more time, then the man went headfirst into the wharf.

Sam walked the few paces to his car to phone headquarters. One of his problems was that while he was a good alley fighter, he was a bad liar. He had been told in so many words from his superiors that if he had to bash the skulls of hoods would he please carry a weapon, to insert into their pockets so it would at least look like self-defense. He never did. It was bad enough to consider a lie, inconceivable to carry one.

But this time, he didn't have to lie too much. He was attacked three against one. He picked up the mike, and for one moment he let his breath come back to him.

He did not see the large van with the reinforced metal grid, set in front like a battering ram. He did not hear it slowly move forward. Sam radioed the sergeant, and was reporting how he tried to save one man from two and how they all three turned on him, when the squad car screeched forward. Instinctively he rammed the brakes. But the scream of his tires told him they were holding. It wasn't the brakes. Behind his car, a large van was slowly pushing his car forward. Then it stopped, backed off, and with increased speed smashed into the rear of the squad car, sending Sam's forehead into the model of Miss Piggy and then into the windshield, and the whole works went plunging off the pier into the dark waters with the radio voice of the sergeant screaming at him, asking what was wrong.

The car paused only briefly before it sank into the putrid darkness. Sam tried to open the door, but it was locked. Someone, somehow, had locked it. He was going down and the world was getting dark. He did not see the frogmen scramble to the door, nor feel them strap an oxygen mask on his face. He did not see them put the corpse in his place, the body of a man whose face had been smashed to a pulp as though an accident had done it.

If the body had not been recovered from the police car with Patrolman Makin's wallet in its pocket, badge on his lapel, the county coroner might have checked the fingerprints; might have, if the fingers hadn't been so damaged in the accident. And if it wasn't so dreadfully obvious what had killed Patrolman Makin the coroner might have done further tests, tests that would have indicated the victim had been dead for an hour before the accident, and that a large brain cancer had claimed his life, not the East River.

But here was the smashed-in face, here was the water over the uniform, and because there was no water in the lungs, the coroner labeled it not death by drowning, but by concussion.

Patrolman Sam Makin was dead.

And a day and a half later he came to and remembered it all.

"Why did you kill me?" asked Sam.

"Because we needed Remo Williams."

"Who is Remo Williams?"

"You're going to save the country, sweetheart. And a live man couldn't possibly do it."

"Who is Remo Williams?"

"You are," said the man who called himself

Con McCleary, the man who would later tell him he had driven the truck that sent his police car into the river. "You are. Here. Let me help you see yourself."

He removed the bandages around the head. And held up a mirror for the patient to see. The cheekbones were higher, the lips thinner and the nose straightened in such a way as to become strong and dominant. The bandages had not been for a head wound. Someone had given him a new face.

"That's not me," said Sam. "I don't know him."

"Remo, you never looked so good," said McCleary.

"Where's my face? What did you do with me?"

"Remo, don't worry about the past. You may even have a future," said McCleary. "I happen to like that face better. And I chose the name myself; don't you like it?"

"Why, certainly. There's nothing quite like being killed and waking up as someone else."

"Remo, you will get to know and love your name. You'll find out it is who you always should have been. Remo, you're going to save our country, or . . ."

"Or what?"

"Well, you know we can always fill a coffin," said the well-dressed black man. "And Sam Makin is already dead."

2

His name was Chiun. But in the village, the village of Sinanju, they called him Master. This day after so long, there was celebration again in the village on the West Korea Bay. Gongs clanged, women dressed in their most decorative kimonos and children were given sweet cakes. For this day, after several decades, the reigning Master was going forth again, as his forefathers had over the centuries, to earn tribute for the House of Sinanju.

Famines might come to other villages on the Korean peninsula, but not the little fishing village of Sinanju, for even if the fish failed to swim into the nets, this village would always eat. Just one jewel or trunk of gold from the House of Sinanju would feed everyone for years. And there were many trunks of gold, and many jewels, in that great house.

Foreign soldiers might come to other villages on the Korean peninsula, taking the women, humiliating the men, but never in Sinanju. The Japanese had ruled Korea. The Chinese had ruled

Korea. But not one of those soldiers dared set foot in Sinanju lest their emperor have them beheaded.

For if a soldier might not know of the power of the House of Sinanju, the king did. The emperor did. The tyrant did. From ancient Rome to the thrones of Japan, from Greek conquerors to Mogul lords, all knew no ruling throat was so regally protected as to be beyond the awesome hands of the Masters of Sinanju.

For centuries, the Masters of Sinanju were assassins to the great. Their services had decided dynasties, felled kingdoms.

So great was the skill of the Masters of Sinanju that others invariably tried to copy them, and invariably failed. Their failures were called Karate, Tai Kwan Do, Ninja, and all the lesser forms of hand fighting imitating the sun source of all the martial arts, Sinanju. And like the weaker rays, they were less than one-hundredth of the source.

For Sinanju was Sinanju and it could never be taken, but only given, and lo for centuries upon centuries it had been given from one Master of Sinanju to another, each going forth into the world to bring back tribute and prosperity to the village . . . until the bad times.

This was the year of the horse, shortly after the turn of one of the western centuries. A great war broke out among white nations, the first of two in which all of them went mad, bringing their wars to Asia also. They were the world wars.

Kings fell. And nations changed. Millions were killed, crudely killed, by anyone calling himself a soldier or general. And nations took it upon themselves to create their own assassins, from whoever lived within their borders, not recognizing that a truly professional assassin could not be made from just anyone or by anyone.

And for years, no one called upon Sinanju for its services.

Until the great year of the dragon, when the planets had reached their most auspicious position, a black from the new nation of America, a mere budding two hundred years old, came to offer tribute to the House of Sinanju.

The man's name was McCleary, meaning that his family's name was McCleary, taken as was white custom from the father's side. The first name, Con, was used by intimates. But if both names were used together, then it became the formal address.

All of this was explained by Chiun who knew whites, Chiun the latest Master of Sinanju who said the stars had foretold the return of the whites, and the return of honor to the House of Sinanju. The world would be reminded again about what had been missing from the halls of power for more than a half-century.

Thus it was a day of celebration. Thus the gongs. Thus the sweet cakes, thus the rejoicing as Chiun in a pink-and-lavender presentation kimono descended from the great house on the hill.

Chiun of course had seen it first out in the bay. Shortly thereafter the villagers saw it. A great metal boat rose from underneath the water to take the Master to his first service in more than fifty years. The House of Sinanju was going out into the world again.

On board the USS *Crawfish*, the captain nervously hoisted the American flag above the conning tower of the submarine. These were North

Korean territorial waters and the last boat to get this close to a North Korean shore was captured, the crew tortured and held for a year. This captain not only was in the waters, he was under orders to dock at the fishing piers of the village.

He had questioned the orders three times. And the last affirmation came from someone above the Secretary of Defense. The USS *Crawfish* was to proceed to the little harbor of Sinanju and thereupon board "with utmost respect," to meet one oriental who was "to be called sir at all times," and to offload four sealed trunks. "The submarine will display the American flag at all times, as though entering a friendly port."

The captain had checked that one especially. The final response to the almost desperate inquiries about the accuracy of the orders was:

"This is absolutely correct. You must identify yourself as an American vessel of war at all times, especially when you enter Sinanju."

The captain had protested. "Sinanju is North Korea. You don't get more north than that." He was taken in for a long confidential talk by a civilian. He did not know the civilian. He just knew the man had higher clearance than the moon.

"Look. I can't tell you what is going on because I know even the Secretary of Defense doesn't have clearance on this one. But Sinanju is not just any village. Even when General MacArthur drove up to the Yalu in the Korean War, before the Chinese counterattacked, we were not allowed to enter Sinanju."

"Why not?" the captain had asked.

"I don't know. But I do know that when the Chinese drove us south again, they didn't enter the village either, and more important, and don't say I was the one who gave you this information, even the North Korean state police don't enter it."

"Don't worry about me telling anyone—I won't live to get the chance," said the captain. He remembered this as he approached the old wooden piers with the fishing sampans tied to it. The village was a small collection of huts, a muddy street, and on a low hill a large wooden house of many jutting rooms. The exteriors of the rooms were Greek design, Roman, Mogul, Czarist, French Provincial, English Tudor. A riot of history with nothing connecting them but walls.

It was not the house, however, that interested the captain of the USS *Crawfish*. Beyond the house, in the surrounding gray Korean hills, artillery pieces trained on his submarine. They had been trained on the USS *Crawfish* since it surfaced in the bay. North Korean soldiers, the most virulently anti-American in the world, were manning them. They couldn't miss. The captain saw the shells load into open breeches. He could almost hear the order to fire as the North Korean officers raised their hands.

Then the captain of the USS *Crawfish* heard it. There was a great bustle in the village. There seemed to be some sort of celebration going on, and then the captain saw what they were celebrating. An elderly man, bald but for wisps of white hair, in a pink-and-lavender robe, shuffled down the muddy strip that was the main street of the village. Behind him laboring men carried fourteen brightly colored large steamer trunks that looked as though they had been saved from a vacation in Victorian England. As the old man walked, he gave little bows. Children held cakes aloft.

And in the hills, to the amazement of the captain, the North Korean artillerymen left their guns to bow low, like Moslems in prayer, touching their heads to the ground in adoration.

"Will you get a load of that?" said the captain to the executive officer.

"I saw it. Who is that guy?" asked the executive officer.

"You're not supposed to know," said the captain.

And he ordered the four trunks offloaded. But there was a problem. The trunks were too heavy. No four men could carry them. No six men could even lift them. They would have to be winched out of the hold.

When they touched the deck of the submarine, the whole ship shivered. Only two things were that heavy. Lead and something else. And when the villagers opened the trunks, the captain saw it was the something else. Four trunks of shiny yellow gold, at least a ton and a half per trunk. Six tons of gold, with gold at several hundred dollars an ounce.

The villagers brought it bar by bar to the strange-looking house on the hill. And then they began loading the fourteen quaint steamer trunks onto the sub.

"Excuse me, sir," said the captain, "but fourteen trunks use up quite a bit of space. Do you think, sir, that you might be able to scrape by with a few trunks less?"

"Able?" said the oriental in the lavender-and-pink robes. He had a squeaky voice, like a broken violin whose bow used too much resin.

"Could you, sir?"

"Why do you ask?"

"Because we don't have enough room."

The oriental thought about that a moment,

and then said something in Korean, which the captain did not understand. But shortly, to the captain's horror, he saw villagers hoist up through the conning tower large torpedoes, and with a human chain move them to the shore. The same chain moved the trunks on board, followed by the oriental.

"I can't leave U.S. torpedoes on a North Korean shore."

"I am not come to your new shores that I should be bothered with the problems of boatmen," said Chiun to the captain, and he clapped his hands signaling that the boat should be off.

There was no more insolence from the boatman thereafter. Chiun, Master of Sinanju, had left his village to glorify its name, so long forgotten among dynasties and kingdoms that had been destroyed in the recent turmoils.

"Hi," greeted Con McCleary when the USS *Crawfish* disgorged its passenger to a large pleasure boat just outside American territorial waters. McCleary was the only passenger on the boat. Navy crewmen unloaded the trunks which filled the small boat almost to tipping. Chiun left the submarine with a nod of acknowledgment to the boatman.

"I am sorry I had to pick you up out here, but this whole organization is secret. It's good to see you again, Master of Sinanju."

"I understand secrets," said Chiun. "I am after all an assassin."

"I told upstairs that," said McCleary.

"Ah, your emperor."

"He is not an emperor," said McCleary. The black had an easy grace for his large tough frame yet it was nothing compared to the frail oriental.

Where McCleary easily balanced with the pitch of the boat as it cut through the waves, Chiun seemed to be part of the waves. The boat moved but he didn't.

"Not emperor yet," said Chiun with a knowing smile.

"No. My boss, the head of the outfit, Harold W. Smith, does not want to be emperor."

"I understand," said Chiun. "He only wishes to serve his people."

"Exactly," said McCleary.

"But when the emperor dies he will reluctantly assume the throne. I understand," said Chiun, and enjoyed the pleasant salt air, waiting to see the shoreline of this new country.

"No. No. He will never be emperor. That's not why you are here. You are not here to assassinate someone."

Chiun smiled. "Of course I am here for that. I am not a dentist after all. I am not here to pull teeth."

"No, as we agreed, you will train someone in Sinanju."

"I only train a future Master. That is the only one who can learn Sinanju."

"But I thought you said you could teach Sinanju. I thought that's what we talked about back in the village when we made the arrangement for the gold tribute and the submarine to pick you up."

"You asked if I could teach Sinanju. And I can."

"Good," said McCleary, trying to dismiss his sudden vision of the whole thing coming apart—the entire phony death of the New York City patrolman, all the strings and setups to bring the one right man to the one right trainer—all falling down now because of a misinterpretation. "Good and wonderful," said McCleary with relief. "You can teach Sinanju."

"To a suitable boy from our village," said Chiun.

"But we don't have one. We don't have one of those," said McCleary, all the nasty thoughts coming back with their relatives called consequences.

"I see by your face you are troubled," said Chiun. "Do not be. You have hired the best in all history. You cannot fail. Do not hate yourself because you have failed to find a suitable pupil. I myself with Sinanju have passed over two generations of young men without a suitable heir. That is my worry, not yours. Your worries are over. You have hired Sinanju. Just name your enemy, and his head will be on your palace wall for display at your pleasure."

Con McCleary steadied the boat. Then he steadied himself.

"Master of Sinanju, we have got to use this one man."

"Does he know Sinanju?"

"No."

"Then why use him?"

"It's complicated. It's an American problem. We went to great trouble to find just the right person who could disappear from the face of the earth. We have found the one person who is just right for us. He will solve our problems."

"And who better to solve them than a Master of Sinanju," said Chiun.

"People will recognize you. I mean people do tend to remember pink-and-lavender kimonos. We need someone who is the average-looking sort of Joe Blow. We need a white man."

"Ah," said Chiun. He finally understood. "You

wish that I teach this white man so that he will teach others, and then you will not have to pay future tribute. This does not work. Genghis Khan tried that with his Mongol horsemen who, you must admit, are far closer to us racially than you are. And they could only ride their ponies better. You have paid for the best, use the best."

"Master, we not only need you to train this one person, we need you to teach him the natural kill or accidental kill as I have heard it described."

"Oh no. You don't want the natural kill. No one knows vengeance has been wreaked when you use the natural kill. A natural kill can look like a fire or a heart attack. It is not something one uses for every occasion."

"Well, that's what we need."

Chiun thought a moment. "There are occasions when a natural kill is warranted. If you are the son of the emperor and you wish to assume the throne, we heartily recommend the natural kill. There are many advantages here. For one, the populace can still believe in the divine right of succession to the throne. In that case the natural kill is not only recommended, it is virtually mandatory. Is your Harold W. Smith the son of an emperor?"

"No. He is just an employee of this country that we both love."

"I see," said Chiun. "Smith is hiring me for the emperor's son."

"No. You are being hired to train someone in Sinanju, with a specialty in the accidental kill."

"I see," said Chiun. He smiled. Of course the man was lying to him. That could be expected especially of a servant who was not of a royal house himself. Eventually, he would come to understand the wisdom of his choice in purchasing the services of the best.

"In any case," said Chiun, "I congratulate you on your choice of the finest assassins of all time. Use us well and we will serve you well and you will have many happy years of reign."

The shoreline of America came into view. It was very green and there were many houses, many like palaces back in Korea. This, claimed the black McCleary, was a shoreline inhabited by commoners, such fine houses being the property of many Americans.

"You see, we are a democracy. We live by laws. But sometimes these laws, meant to protect us, make this country's survival almost impossible. The laws are meant to keep the people who live in these houses safe. Unfortunately, they also protect the enemies of the country. The law protects the criminal element from the law, so to speak."

Chiun smiled. Any fool would know that whatever an emperor did was the law itself. The dark-skinned white man was hinting at imperial ineptitude. There was a plot afoot in this land of many houses.

"So sometimes special measures need to be taken. Things must be done outside the law. And they have to be very secret because we can't afford to admit our laws just don't work in protecting us. We do the special things; me, and Smith, and the man you will train named Remo."

Chiun nodded. An emperor only had to be secretive when planning to betray another emperor. But if it pleased this servant of the emperor to concoct fairy tales until the true motives were admitted, Chiun could accept that.

The Master of Sinanju had already been paid. The emperor's truth was now Chiun's truth, as well—at least until his job was done.

3

The face in the mirror was not his face. The name on the bed chart was not his name. He would have thought he was going crazy if not for the scar from the baseball bat. He had been hit with the bat on the pier, and the blows broke skin. Despite the pain of the plastic surgery, he could feel the pull of the stitches that closed the wound.

And all that told Sam he had been set up on the wharf for this thing that he had been shanghaied into. All those psychological tests, and even being kept on the shift two hours longer so that he would be there in the squad car when the first man fled from the other two. Of course all three were part of the same team, setting up his death.

The nurse called him Remo, and Con McCleary called him Remo, and this morning somebody was going to tell him what it was all about.

"I am not Remo Williams," he told the nurse before McCleary got there.

"I understand, Remo," she said. "Concussions can do that."

She had light brown hair, a full bosom stretching her white uniform, and a presence that let him know if he weren't on his back nude in bed, she might be.

"Look, sweetheart, would it shock you if I told you my name is Sam Makin? I am a policeman who was killed . . . I guess two days ago. I don't even know what day it is."

"It's Wednesday, Remo."

"Would it shock you if I told you that I wasn't Remo but someone who was killed in New York City?"

"No. That is a natural response to escaping death. A sense of guilt for having survived so intense that you identify with someone who didn't. It's quite natural, Remo. And you'll get over it."

"Can I have my clothes?"

"You don't need your clothes, Remo. You're recovering."

"All right then, what did you do with my clothes? Don't you see, I am being kept a prisoner here without clothes."

"I assure you, Remo, you will get over those feelings of being a prisoner."

"Nurse. Get me some clothes or the sheet comes off," he said. She laughed. He ripped the sheet off his body and stood nude facing her.

"You seem to forget, I'm a nurse," she said.

He shrugged. She was right.

"But let me give you my phone number," she said, looking over his body. "I am also a woman."

"Get me a pair of pants," he said. "I'll take them off in your apartment."

She laughed. "Remo, you're a card."

It dawned on him then that as Remo Williams, the man who didn't exist, he could punch her in the back of that laughing head and not commit a crime. Dead men did not commit crimes. They couldn't. And suddenly a large part of the whole scheme came clear to him. As Remo Williams he could kill without committing a crime. This was the advantage he'd been given, the advantage somebody wanted him to have. Badly. But if he could physically kill this grinning man who so happily claimed he set up the whole thing, McCleary, then there would be no charge against Sam Makin. Sam Makin was dead.

All right, he would be Remo Williams for a while. To kill if he had to.

He was smiling when Con McCleary returned that afternoon, saying he had been busy that morning picking up someone off the coast.

"How are you doing, Remo?"

"Fine," said Remo. The name did not feel half bad once he got used to it. Of course, the once was still a while away. "Today is the day you tell me what this is all about."

"You seem more cheerful today."

"What have I got to lose?" said Remo. He smiled.

McCleary smiled. "Pretty abrupt turnabout. Your psych profile said you would come over, but not this fast. But I say to hell with psych profiles, right?"

"Right," said Remo. He could see that under McCleary's plaid jacket was a tip of a shoulder holster. He could grab that gun, shoot McCleary in the face and then run. They couldn't charge the man who didn't exist. Remo offered McCleary all that remained of his hospital lunch—Jell-O. McCleary shook his head.

"You're here because America is in trouble. Too many of our cops are corrupt. Too many of our judges, corrupt. Too many of our politicians are for sale."

"So what else is new?" said Remo.

"That's where you come in. You're going to be the eleventh commandment. Thou shalt not get away with it."

"I see. So you created a man who can kill without committing a crime. A man who doesn't exist."

"For an organization that doesn't exist, Remo. But that's another story. You get well first."

"Let me ask you another question. Who gave you your name?"

"My name's always been McCleary. It's my father's name."

"How come you get to keep your name?"

"Because I am nothing special. You are going to be the deadliest white man ever to set foot on this earth. You are going to be our killer arm. There is a lot of work for you, laddie."

Remo was quiet.

"But you're not deadly now. You're just a New York cop with a changed face, and some smarts. Right now I am tougher and smarter than you are, laddie. So lay back. Enjoy the food. Bang that busty nurse if you want, and wait for the good things."

"What could be better than being drowned?" asked Remo.

McCleary laughed and gave him a little playful punch in the shoulder. McCleary's hand felt funny. Stiff.

"Say, what's the name of this place anyway? Where am I?"

"You're in good hands, Remo," said McCleary. And he laughed. "Fear not the valley of death, Remo. Because you are going to be the toughest sonuvabitch in it."

Remo laughed too. If that should ever happen, McCleary was going to be the first to regret it.

He found out from the nurse that the hospital was in New York State, thirty miles north of the city. He found out they did operations, and had a large convalescent wing. He noticed his window was barred. She said that was some sort of clerical error. This was a mental-patient wing and he was obviously not mental. While she couldn't give him street clothes, she certainly could provide a hospital gown. Did Remo want her to put it on for him?

He said yes. She locked the door. Then she showed him a very interesting way to dress a patient. She put the gown on him with her lips and tongue. It took thirty minutes.

"Was it good for you?" she asked.

He said it was. He wondered how she did with overcoats and slacks, and socks and shoes. She giggled. When she left, Remo waited until it was dark, until the first bedcheck, and then quietly, in bare feet, walked out into the corridor. The problem was clothes. If he lifted some from a patient he ran the risk of being caught. On the mental ward that could become unpleasant. But the operating room, where doctors dressed in hospital gowns . . . Where there were surgeons, there were unused slacks, shirts and jackets, and maybe even shoes.

He stole a mask from a fresh pile of laundry, and with mask over face found the surgeons' lounge, then strolled in as though he had every right to be there. One trusting soul, apparently saving someone's life in a nearby operating room, had left his locker open. He had a fine suit, with a good silk shirt, and the best tie Remo ever had around his neck. He left the watch. Even though he couldn't legally commit a crime, he still didn't believe in stealing.

He left the hospital through the front entrance, and waited for an ambulance. One arrived just as he needed it. The stars were smiling on him. When the driver hopped out to assist an elderly wheelchair patient out of the rear, Remo hopped in. The driver shut the door. Remo floored the accelerator and sped out of the hospital compound. He was giddy with success. He almost laughed. What incredible freedom. He could go anywhere. Do anything. Be anything. He was the freest man ever created.

Right up until the snub-nosed .38 pressed against his ear.

"Hi, Remo," said McCleary. "You're right on time. Make a left turn at the next intersection."

"You wouldn't kill me after you went to all that trouble to get me," said Remo.

"What else could we do with you if you won't work for us?" said McCleary. The man might not be nice, but he was reasonable.

Remo made the left turn at the next intersection. There was a sign indicating they were heading for New York City.

"You are not yet the toughest sonuvabitch in the valley, Remo."

"When I am, you're dead, McCleary," said Remo into the barrel of the snub-nosed pistol.

"Ah, laddie. You're going to have to wait on line. And there'll be a line waiting for you, too. Don't worry. It happens when you're on the side of the good."

Remo spit at the gun. McCleary didn't fire. He laughed and holstered the weapon under his shoulder.

Traffic at two A.M. was scarce anywhere, but in

the financial district of New York City, where McCleary guided him, it was nonexistent. The giant buildings of commerce were as still as tombstones. Remo, on McCleary's instructions, parked in front of a fifty-story bank with lots of dark glass, stretching upward with all the creative imagination of a box.

"A bank?" said Remo. "You rearranged my face so I can work for a bank?"

"Hell no. Some of them are the biggest crooks."

"Then what are we doing here? Are you going to open up an account for me?"

"Come on. Inside. You're going to find out everything here."

The room Remo was supposed to find out everything in was filled with computers. A lemony-faced man in a vest with rimless glasses and pursed lips sat at a terminal, though his version of sitting defied the definition of the word. There was no relaxation in his position. His back was ruler straight, his neck rigid, his hands tense. It was as though he was arm-wrestling the terminal.

"Where's his boss?" said Remo.

"That is the boss," said McCleary. "Harold W. Smith."

Smith did not turn around.

"Then why is he at the computer? Bosses sit behind desks."

"Not this one. And these are not just any computers."

Remo glanced over the man's shoulder. Pictures appeared on the screen. Pictures of police files, an agricultural bulletin, IRS reports. And on closer scrutiny Remo noticed something else of interest. Each of the messages being transmitted was destined for some department bigwig. The IRS was reporting to a district office. The police sending information thought they were addressing the FBI. An agricultural report appeared to be going to some undersecretary. These reports were being filed as though they were just routine office procedures. Because that's what the lackeys who sent them believed they were.

"They don't know who they are reporting to, do they?" said Remo.

"No," said Smith. The word was even sharper than usual, cut with the hard vowels of New England. "They don't." He nodded to the computers. "This is who we are. We oversee operations and make little adjustments. You would be surprised at how good these programs are at spotting it when something is fishy. Then we notify the proper people to investigate. It's the added little help the country needs."

"And who is notified when someone is kidnapped, operated on to change his face, and faked in death? Who is notified then?" said Remo.

"We really didn't have much other choice in recruiting," said Smith.

"Recruiting? You dumped me in the river and reshuffled my face and you call it recruiting?"

"Would you have volunteered?"

"Hell no."

"Well, then consider it being drafted in a time of national emergency. And America is in an emergency, Mr. Williams. Let me show you how we work."

"I've seen the way you work. You run black-bag operations. You kidnap people. You beat the shit out of them, and nobody holds you accountable."

"Oh, we're accountable, son."

"Let me guess," said Remo. "To the President?"

"To this one as well as the five before him,"

said Smith. Remo noticed Smith's vest wasn't even wrinkled. The green-and-black tie was tight under Smith's neck and it might have been that way since dawn the previous day. Only the eyes showed the strain.

"Good. Then tell them you made a mistake in your draft."

"Your profile says we haven't. But I am not here to argue with you. I am going to go through this once, Mr. Williams, and then . . . and then I expect you will understand."

Smith removed a pipe from the inside of his gray jacket that matched his gray vest and his gray pants, set beneath that lemony face that mirrored his obviously gray soul. Smith stoked the pipe with tobacco, lit it, and then nodded to the computer terminal.

"We live under the greatest social document the world has ever known. The United States Constitution. It protects citizens as no document protects citizens. Unfortunately, years ago, it became apparent that the country was going through troubled times. It might not survive, not while adhering to the wonderful document that really is America, the Constitution. What to do? Remove the rights of people? Possibly. But then we become like every other country that has gone down the drain in an effort to establish law and order. And then a President, now dead, had an idea. Instead of taking away citizens' rights, why not create an organization that could infiltrate the personal sector to oversee the areas of strategic importance to the country? Yes, it would violate the laws, but it would not be acknowledged. It would never have official sanction. And it would only exist for the few dangerous years and then quietly slide into oblivion. Are you following me?"

Remo was quiet. He glanced at McCleary. McCleary was watching him, but this time there were no sensors attached to Remo's wrists.

"This organization would get America through the troubled times. And our country would emerge safe and with the laws still intact. Do you see now why we needed an organization that didn't exist? The very admission of its existence would mean we weren't America anymore."

If Remo had a watch, he would have looked at it.

"This is a precious country, Remo. Many have died for it. Many have vilified it, but this is still the land people escape to, not from. And if I had any other choice, I would not have recruited you this way."

"Uh-huh," said Remo. "Look, is there a place I can get a bite to eat?"

Smith cleared his throat. "In any case, we found we needed someone special."

"A killer. You needed a killer."

"Ah, so you have figured that part out," said Smith.

"What happens when all those agencies realize they are reporting to someone illegal, or at least that someone illegal has access to their secrets?"

"I thought you noticed that. That's why I let you look over my shoulder. They don't know whom they're working for. Eighty-five percent of all the people in every job do not know what they are doing. Even the smart fifteen percent can be fooled. They don't know where reports go. Sadly, the highest percentage don't care where their information goes."

"So who does know?"

"You. Me. McCleary. And each President."

"That's it?"

"It," said Smith.

If I kill these two, thought Remo, I am home free. What is the President going to do? Claim the man his secret organization kidnapped has committed murder? Hell, I can kill these two.

And then as though the fates that had denied him a mother and father were making up for all of it, McCleary handed Remo a pistol.

"It's for you. You've got your first hit tonight. We are a busy, busy group. You are our muscle. I told you you were going to save this country, laddie," said McCleary.

Remo took the gun, and because McCleary had offered it handle-forward, let the barrel sit facing McCleary for a moment. McCleary only thought that was humorous. Remo couldn't shoot a smiling man, and besides, he didn't have to.

"Okay," said Remo. "I'll try a hit."

"Good," said Smith.

"Good," said McCleary, and he was laughing.

"What are you laughing at?" said Remo.

"You're such a good boy," said McCleary, and he gave Remo a friendly pinch on the cheek. Remo gave a friendly shove of the heel of his hand into McCleary's chin.

Smith shook his head. "Gentlemen, please."

"Smitty doesn't mind the fighting so much as the idea that someone might be enjoying himself. He's from an old New England family. They don't trust us midwesterners, and they don't trust you, laddie, to know everything. Just their own. I think his ancestors came over on the *Mayflower*."

Smith looked at his watch.

"I didn't ask that you wait until the target dies of old age," he said. "Good day, Remo. And good hunting."

McCleary had new clothes waiting for Remo,

even a wallet with money and credit cards for Remo Williams, along with a driver's license.

"You never have to worry about money. That's a plus," said McCleary.

Remo gave him the usual smile in lieu of saying drop dead.

There was a new car also. McCleary drove Remo into the West Side of New York City. Remo wondered if he would ever return to Brooklyn, just to look at his old apartment. But he thought not. That belonged to a dead man. And besides, there was more cash in his wallet now than he had been worth as a New York City patrolman.

The car stopped in front of a three-story brownstone, just north of Harlem and west of Central Park. A crack of red dawn was coming up between the buildings behind them. The street smelled of uncollected garbage.

"He's in there. The first floor. Don't take any chances. Go in. Put the gun in his face, and fire. Okay?"

"Right," said Remo.

"Don't be fooled by what he looks like." McCleary's voice was hushed. "And look, fella. There was nothing personal in any of this. I want you to know that. The computer picked you."

"The first floor?" said Remo.

"Right," said McCleary. He hasn't laughing now.

Remo left the car and shut the door noiselessly. His mouth was dry. He felt the handle of the door. It was unlocked. He pushed it forward. His feet were quiet. He went forward. The inner door opened with a touch. He entered a hallway. A door was open at the other end. He went forward. The room was lit. An old man knelt before a table. He was painting. Wisps of white hair fell over his parchment-yellow skin. He was an oriental. He looked up.

"Speakee English?" asked Remo.

The oriental was quiet, his head set regally as though looking at a supplicant who had made himself too humble. There was an annoyance about the man.

"Does a nightingale sing?" answered the old man. Remo didn't want to hurt him.

"Is there a way out of here?" asked Remo.

"You may leave the way you entered," said the oriental.

"Listen. There is someone out there who wants me to kill your boss."

"Boss? I have no boss. I am not a slave, or a worker."

"Well, who else is here?"

"Else? Else? I am here."

"Look, I don't want to make any trouble for you, I have nothing against you, and I have no intention of killing you. I don't want to kill anyone. I just want to get out of here."

"Kill me?" said the oriental. With delicacy he put down the brush he had been writing with. He rose.

The oriental's flowered kimono glistened in the lamplight. He moved with such quiet it appeared as though he floated. But he did the one thing an ex-patrolman could not let him do. He reached inside the kimono, and before a gun could come out, Remo fired.

Outside Con McCleary heard a shot. Then three more. A patrol car pulled up, checking out the noise. McCleary flashed a badge and identification.

"Check with your precinct. This is a joint Secret Service/FBI stakeout. You can't enter. That's federal property."

"Oh, that's the house," said one of the patrolmen.

"That's the house," said McCleary, and turned off the engine, got out of the car, and entered the brownstone. There was silence inside. McCleary walked very carefully.

Inside, Remo almost strangled the handle of the Colt. Remo knew it fired. He saw the flash. He knew it wasn't firing blanks. He felt the kick. He saw the table behind the oriental shatter. There was the oriental, there was the barrel of the gun, there was the squeeze of the trigger, there was the shot. And bang. A lamp went. He shot at the man's head. A plaster wall spat out a shower of white dry cloud. He unloaded the gun at an elderly man he couldn't possibly miss in a small room, and all he accomplished was to shoot up the furniture and wall. And the old man in that absurdly glaring robe had hardly even moved. Just enough each time so that the head or body was not there to meet the bullet.

And the old oriental moved like a nightmare. It did not seem that he was fast, but that Remo was slow. Somehow every previously adequate movement was made to seem a form of slow motion.

The old man had fingernails that looked as though they would break in a breeze, long and curving like quills. But the fingernails seized the gun, turned it around, and Remo wondered whether there was another bullet in the chamber. He looked at the barrel. And then he heard the remaining bullets fall to the floor as the old man stripped the magazine and discarded the pistol with contempt.

Remo threw a punch. He almost threw out his shoulder. He felt his arm being straightened.

"No. No," said the oriental. "You smash. You crush. No. Why do you do these things?"

"I want to kill you," gasped Remo.

"That's not a way to kill anyone," said the oriental. "You couldn't kill a fly, you impertinent piece of duck dung."

Remo threw another punch. That missed. Then he threw his arms around the man who could be no more than five feet tall, and weigh no more than ninety-five pounds. Remo would just drop him to the floor, and then let him wriggle out from under two hundred pounds. Take away his speed. Remo's arms went flying back as if blown there by a hurricane wind, yet he could swear that the frail little old man did not move.

Remo saw the grinning face of McCleary enter the room. He threw a punch at McCleary's chest. He was surprised that it landed. He had become used to missing. McCleary went back against the wall with a thud.

McCleary groaned and reached for the large numb spot on his chest. Remo felt himself put down on a chair, guided by one of those incredibly frail fingernails.

"Don't encourage him by allowing yourself to be hit like that," said the oriental to McCleary.

"He's got quite a punch," said McCleary.

"Even a pebble falls like a mountain into goose down."

"Well, Chiun, Master of Sinanju, what do you think of him?"

"He bangs. He clubs. But all white men think like that," said Chiun.

"Do you think you can do anything with him?" asked McCleary.

"He is very slow, and clumsy and poorly coordinated."

"He's got one of the best nerve-time responses in the country. We tested for that, Master of Sinanju."

"Among whites?"

"Among whites and blacks," said McCleary.

"Well, if this is your best, this is your best."

"What do you think?"

"He moves like a baboon with two club feet. But he moves."

"What does that mean?" asked McCleary.

"It means we will do what we can," said Chiun.

"What about me?" said Remo.

"We're talking about you," said Chiun.

"What about my feelings?" said Remo. "What about what I intend to do?"

"You might try gratitude," said Chiun. "Do you know who I am?"

"I know who this sonuvabitch is," said Remo, pointing to McCleary. "And if this is another trick, McCleary, I will get you."

"That's a yes, then?" said McCleary.

Chiun, Master of Sinanju, listened in stunned amazement. Here was someone about to be given personally, from a Master himself, the sun source of all man's physical powers, and there was question over whether he would take it. Chiun wondered whether these whites would have to be begged to accept a mountain of gold.

"I dunno," said Remo. "What else am I going to do? I could run, maybe get away. I think I could use what this Jap has to teach me. I have no place else to go. Right now, McCleary."

"You're doing right, Remo."

"Can I change my name back? Or choose another?"

"Try Remo for a while. See how it hangs."

"No promises. I'm just going to give it a shot."

McCleary rubbed his chest and grinned. "As for our promises, we will be able to give you terror for breakfast, pressure for lunch and aggravation for sleep. Your vacations are two minutes when you're not looking over your shoulder. If you live to draw a pension, it will be a miracle."

"Are there any disadvantages?" asked Remo.

"You'll do all right, Remo. You're the right man for the job. He's all yours, Chiun."

"Do I have to live with him?" asked Remo.

"In the Orient, that would be considered an honor," said McCleary.

Chiun wondered what they were talking about. He was, of course, the first to discover this new nation of American whites, and he had already noted they seemed exceptionally rich and exceptionally crazy. Therefore the white called Remo could be forgiven for mistaking Chiun for a Japanese.

The one thing the Master of Sinanju did not mention to either of them was perhaps the most important thing of all. He was surprised to see it in a white. Yet, there it was in the eyes of the meat-smelling fat white named Remo. You could only see it when a man was fighting for his life. It was not anger. Anger was only fear with a different face. It was that shining, that very cold and very distant shining like a star far off in the universe. Chiun wondered what a white man was doing with it and he wondered if there were more like this Remo. Was this an accident of birth, or the work of the universe?

This observation was too great a secret to share with anyone; it had to be held close. He would have to find out who this white's parents were. But first, there was so much work to do.

4

Harold W. Smith returned the next morning at eight o'clock, having allowed himself three hours' sleep. The computer had spit out a judge's name. He had the lowest prison-sentence record in the country, and one of the fastest-growing real-estate holdings. The computer was programmed to coordinate such things. In fact, Smith didn't even have to tell an FBI office to look into it. The computer did that automatically.

But he was not thinking about corrupt judges this morning. After years of struggle they now had their killer arm, a man who would end helplessness in certain areas, areas in which some got away with crimes because they shot away witnesses. Terror would be met with terror. If it worked.

Con McCleary ambled into the headquarters at the Wall Street bank about one P.M. with beer on his breath.

"How is it going?" asked Smith.

"Fine. The beer's good. The women are willing. I love New York."

"You know what I mean."

"Oh, Remo and the Master of Sinanju. Wonderful. Fine. That's why I am celebrating."

"That's a little premature, isn't it?" asked Smith.

"I am celebrating the fact that Remo said yes and Chiun said yes."

"I still have my doubts. I don't believe in the effectiveness of karate. A bullet travels much faster. And electronic devices travel a lot faster than that."

"But we can't leave anything that would be traced. We need a hand killer."

"Yes," said Smith. "That's why I agreed. Agreed to everything."

"Don't be so glum," said McCleary. "The old man can dodge bullets."

"I'd have to see it to believe it."

"You'll believe," said McCleary. "Those assassins live in legends of the east for centuries, thousands of years. There are even references to them in western courts. Did you know they stopped Alexander the Great because he killed a client of theirs, Darius, the Persian emperor?"

"That's history," said Smith, returning to the computer.

"History," said McCleary, "is made up of lots of todays that just aren't here anymore."

"Go back to your beer," said Smith. "We're committed, but not happily."

"But then again, you're never happy," said McCleary.

But Smith was not listening to him. Something very strange was happening in an especially sensitive part of America's defenses. The organization's computers were sounding an alarm. They were having difficulty accessing areas they were normally supposed to monitor. It was as though entire crucial areas of America's defense system were off limits to American scrutiny. At first, Smith thought this had to be some form of computer error.

"First, show me how you do that thing with the bullets. You know, the dodging," said Remo.

He sat on a bare wood floor in a well-lit room stripped of anything but bamboo mats spread along the two farthest walls. Those were for sleeping, Remo was told. Next door was another room, with fourteen steamer trunks that seemed to have enough colored kimonos to furnish a decade of oriental fashion shows. Chiun seemed to have one appropriate for each moment of the day and for each purpose of each moment.

"That is not first," said Chiun.

"Was it hypnotism?" said Remo.

"Are you going to learn or are you going to talk?"

"The best way to learn is to ask questions," said Remo.

The room was cold. But Chiun did not seem to mind cold. Nor did he react to the heat when the big iron radiators steamed up.

"And how do you know the best way to learn?"

"Well, we were taught that."

"Which is why you know nothing. The best way to learn is to listen to him who knows. I know. You do not know. Listen."

"What if I don't understand something?"

"Of course you don't understand, that is why you are learning. You will learn better if I talk and you do not, because I know and you do not know."

Remo shrugged. His legs hurt, being tucked

under one another as he sat in what Chiun had called the sitting-alert position, best for learning.

"The first thing you must realize is that a gun is not the best weapon."

"Right. Your hands," said Remo.

"Your hands are not your greatest weapon, nor are your legs, or even, as you will learn, your breathing. The greatest weapon on this earth is your mind. The cheetah is faster. The gorilla stronger. And of course a bird can fly. But man rules because he has his mind."

Chiun paused. "Of the ten places of the mind, man uses less than one. This was discovered by the Great Master Go, the Elder, in your year of 1200 B.C., dating from the emergence of your God."

"I'm not religious," said Remo. "But you know I once read that modern scientists have discovered that we use only eight percent of our minds. Did you know that?"

Chiun folded his gray morning kimono around his long fingers and sat down in the learning position. He was quiet.

"I just wanted you to know that," said Remo after a while. "I thought you might find it interesting."

After another while when Chiun did not speak, Remo said:

"Okay. I am sorry. I will listen."

Chiun rose. He raised a finger.

"First, you must realize you made a horrible mistake, one that I can only forgive once."

Remo felt his legs begin to hurt, tucked under him in a lotus position. He moved around. He was quiet.

"You called me a Japanse. I am not Japanese. There is a story about peoples. Whites have light skin to make up for the cold climates in which they live. That is one aberration. Blacks have dark skin to make up for the heat in which they grew. That is the second aberration. But yellow men have the color that is perfect and normal. They are no aberration.

"Yet, among yellow men, the Japanese are perfidious. The Chinese lazy. The Thai slow. The Cambodian demented, the Burmese peculiar in the extreme, and not just a little bit gluttonous.

"Only the Korean can claim diligence, courage, intelligence, beauty and perfection. But I am sorry to say, not all Koreans have these virtues. The southerners are too emotional, and north we find decadence in Pyongyang. Only in the blessed village of Sinanju do we find people worthy of being what mankind should be. Except of course the fishermen who have become lazy because of the generosity of the House of Sinanju and the baker who cheats on weights, and at times the women can be hard."

"You're Korean, aren't you?" said Remo.

Chiun smiled. "See. You listen and you learn."

"And you're from Sinanju," said Remo.

"You are learning."

The second, and next most important, lesson was breathing. Remo thought it was idiotic.

"I've always breathed," said Remo. "Everybody who is alive breathes. They do it from birth and stop at death."

"And they do it wrong. Like you. Like the way you happened to start at birth, never bothering to give it another thought, unless you have a problem with it. Willy-nilly. Breath. When you are exhausted you breathe hard. When you are frightened you hold your breath. But you never let it give you the power of your most important fuel. Air. You will start now to breathe correctly."

Remo felt Chiun's fingernails straighten his spine and press his diaphragm and then release. He felt the air go deeper into his lungs. He felt a calmness come over him. Suddenly his mouth was filled with the odor of rancid fat.

"Where'd that come from?" asked Remo. "Who has left meat to rot?"

"You have, in your last meal. The meat is rotting in your stomach. You eat dead meat."

"That reminds me. I'm hungry. I haven't eaten since last night," said Remo.

"So you ate," said Chiun. "And besides you are too fat. You move like a pregnant yak. Live off your stored fat for a while."

"I'm hungry," said Remo. "And I am not going to sit around here breathing and starving to death waiting for you to show me how to break some board with my bare hands. I've done your breathing; now let's get on with the training."

Remo saw the finger. He saw the long nail of Chiun go forward. He saw it touch his bicep. And then he felt as though someone had dropped a safe on that bicep. His arm was broken. He was sure his arm was broken. He rolled on the floor and groaned in pain.

So close to the floor he could see the grain in the wood, he nursed his injured arm with the other, and heard Chiun speak.

"You did not ask to be here, I gather. No more than you asked to be white, or arrogant, or insolent. It is not your fault. So let us make this agreement. I will train. You will learn. And then I will leave."

"Yeah. Yeah. Okay. Okay. But how am I going to learn with a broken arm?"

Remo felt the fingernail touch the bicep again and then there was no pain. He moved the arm.

He stretched it. He turned it. He felt it with the other hand. Miraculously the bone had been restored.

"How did you fix the break?"

"If you will listen," said Chiun, "you will understand that bones and muscle do not make strength. Nerves make strength. Knowledge makes strength. The mind you do not use can make strength. The arm was never broken. It only had to feel like it was broken for you to listen to me. He who talks cannot listen."

"Do you always talk like a Chinese fortune cookie?" asked Remo.

He saw the fingernail again, but this time he was ready to dodge it. Strangely it seemed almost attached to him, one with him, until the pain came to his solar plexus. Then after sufficient groveling on the floor that pain was released.

"Okay," gasped Remo. "Korean cookie."

Chiun nodded.

"You bastard," said Remo.

"That is swear word, a curse of sorts. Swearing is a helplessness. You are not here to learn to be helpless."

Learning to breathe was harder than Remo thought. Chiun kept blaming it on Remo's immoral life.

"You grunt. You groan because of the poisons you have brought into your system," said Chiun.

"It would help if you stopped standing on my stomach," said Remo.

Every breath had to raise Chiun. The slippers were firm in his abdomen.

"Let the muscles go. You are holding me with your muscles."

"Otherwise you'll sink."

"Raise me with the breathing. Feel the floor you are on. Sense the floor. Sense the air. Sense yourself. Be yourself. Breathe."

Remo let the stomach muscles go, and at first tensed to keep Chiun's weight from collapsing his stomach. But as soon as he thought of his breathing, sensed the air, even the dust in it, and the light in it, he felt he could breathe with lightness, as though the man standing on him was part of him, and breathing was right and steady. He did not feel the weight of Chiun on him or off him. His body understood. His breathing knew. He tasted light and darkness with his breathing.

One did not need eyes to see, or hands to feel, or even skin to sense the cold and the warm. The breathing made him one with all of it, in space and on the wood floor of this bare room two stories high, with the skylight and the vastness above it. Remo opened his eyes.

It was dark. He looked at Chiun.

"How long was I breathing like that?"

"As long as you needed," said Chiun.

"Eight hours? It felt like a minute."

"Time is something that takes place in the mind of the universe," said Chiun.

"May I ask what you mean by that?"

"No," said Chiun.

"When am I going to learn to dodge bullets and things?"

"You will learn everything you can, and no more than you can," said Chiun. "Now go to sleep."

"I'm hungry," said Remo.

"Use your fat," said Chiun.

"That's not exactly a meal," said Remo.

"I will tell you when you are ready for a meal."

"I'm ready. I'm ready."

"You ate Tuesday. Now quiet," said Chiun.

It became clear in the days that followed that what Remo was learning was not hand fighting as he knew it. Chiun showed him a fingerboard Remo had seen karate students use. Actually, Remo had never seen them use it. Patrolman Sam Makin had seen them use it. The name was bothering him now. He had taken "Remo" assuming he would use it for a day or two, and then be free of everything. Now he dreamed in Sam Makin, and he thought in Remo. Sometimes he thought in Patrolman Sam Makin, and dreamed in Remo. Sometimes he didn't know one from the other. But he always called himself Remo.

He had been in training three weeks, mostly breathing and starving, when Chiun showed him the fingerboard.

Remo tapped the soft pads of his fingers against the wooden board to toughen them. When he was done, Chiun told him to hang it on the wall. Remo asked how. Chiun showed him the proper way to train fingers on a board. Then, with two taps of his index finger, he put a hole in it.

"You build calluses on your fingers but build strength in your mind. You must believe; that is where your strength is. Man is the only animal that does not believe in his own powers."

"I believe. I believe I am hungry. I believe I am Patrolman Sam Makin. I believe I am Remo Williams. I believe. I believe."

"That is not belief, that is anger."

"You should be happy with anger. You're a killer."

Chiun clutched a delicate hand to his bosom.

"This is the second thing you must learn, almost as important as knowing the difference between Koreans and lesser peoples of the naturally colored race.

"I do not train you to kill. A truck kills. Meat of cows kills. A professional assassin promotes harmony and brings about a more peaceful humor to the entire community."

"You make it sound like a public service."

"A professional assassin is the highest public servant," said Chiun, who went on to tell him about the horrors of the last half-century, when governments spurned assassins for amateurs of their own kind.

"Yes, it is true," said Chiun. "Every government seems to have these crude imitations in great number, and what is the result? Mass murder. Killing. They are the killers. When the world returns to the proper assassins you will see grace and harmony."

"I'd like to see breakfast," said Remo. Patrolman Sam Makin used to love breakfast. Sam Makin used to fry brown sausage, and cut onions and butter into steaming rich potatoes. Sam Makin used to spread sweet red jams on crisp rolls.

Even the nuns at the orphanage had allowed Sam Makin to have as many rolls and as much jam as he liked, as well as a hot cereal during the winter that Sam Makin used to call warm cement.

Remo Williams would have given cartilage for that cereal now.

Chiun said Remo did not understand starvation. Starvation was when the body did not get what it needed. Remo did not need food. He needed to memorize the names of the first hundred Masters of Sinanju. He needed to learn how Sinanju came about, how selfless the Masters were. How the world was.

"What do I care how castles are fortified?" asked Remo. "I am never going to crawl into a king's bedroom."

"You think everything you see is new just because you see it for the first time. But everything has been here before. It has just had different names. And they too, in times so far ago no word remains today, thought they were new. But even then, they were not new."

Finally, after weeks and weeks of breathing and moving, and learning about more dead Koreans than Remo thought ever existed, Chiun said Remo was ready to go outside. But he had better leave Sam Makin in the past or he might not survive the day.

Before dawn, Chiun had Remo walk outside with him. Now Chiun wore the dark kimono, which he explained was copied by the Ninja assassins of Japan.

"A nation notorious for cheap imitations," said Chiun. They walked several blocks with Chiun peering into the night sky, looking for something above them. They entered a building with an elevator. Chiun pointed to the elevator doors.

"I like these. I rode in one yesterday," said Chiun. "They're called elevators."

"I know," said Remo. "I was raised in this country."

"Shut your eyes," said Chiun.

Remo did so. They entered the elevator, and Remo called off the floors with his eyes shut, right up to forty, where the elevator stopped. Still with his eyes shut he followed Chiun up a flight of stairs.

"You are now going to learn that one does not

jump with his eyes," said Chiun. "You are going to jump from one place to another with your eyes shut. You will sense me, sense where I land and then you will land there."

"Okay," said Remo. He was smiling. It was fun. It could be fun. Without looking he knew where Chiun was. If he were to be asked in feet and inches he would say Chiun was eight feet, seven inches in front of him. He knew it. And he didn't question it. All of this came from the knowing that was in the air in his lungs with his breath. He had captured the rhythms of the universe, and had joined them.

The floor beneath him was somewhat soft to the footstep. He heard Chiun jump up two feet and land on something hard, hard as concrete. Remo jumped two feet and landed next to Chiun. Chiun moved forward and then jumped horizontally fifteen feet across this concrete floor. Remo stepped, breathed, jumped and landed fifteen feet forward. He could never jump fifteen feet in high school but this wasn't just jumping. This was letting the body move where the mind wished. The body knew so much more about itself than the person did. It all came through the breathing. That which should have been alivc all the time was alive now. And it was simple.

Yet there was a strange feeling as he spanned those fifteen feet; it was as though the concrete had become exceedingly light, very thin, like clouds beneath him. He opened his eyes to find the reason behind that odd lightness, and when he did, he gasped.

"Holy shit," screamed Remo. He was looking down forty stories from the concrete railing of a roof. He had been jumping from one building to another with his eyes closed. He felt his legs give way and, terrified, he reached in toward the dark surface of the rooftop behind him. He fell to it, trembling.

"What is your problem?" asked Chiun. "If that railing were on the ground you would strut across it like a peacock."

"That's forty stories down. It's not on the damned ground. It was never on the damned ground. You had me jump from one building to another with my eyes shut."

"Why are you afraid? Do you want to fall?"

"That is a dumb question," said Remo. The tar on the roof was sticky. That apparently was the softness he felt beneath his feet on the roof he had left before he jumped to the concrete railing. He stood up.

"Answer the question," said Chiun.

"No. I don't want to fall, of course."

"You fall because you are afraid. Fear is nothing more than a feeling. Do not give it more due than it deserves. You feel hot. You feel hungry. You feel angry. You feel afraid. Fear can never kill you. So what are you afraid of?"

"Falling forty stories."

"If you fill your mind with fear, you cannot fill it with the powers you have. And to do that you must breathe. Allow yourself to fall and you will not fall. Up. Come," said Chiun, and beckoned Remo to the railing.

Remo forced himself up on the rail and avoided looking at the streets below.

"Do not tell yourself the fall is not there because your body knows it is a lie. Your body is becoming Sinanju through your mind. Come. It is easy," said Chiun, and backing away in the dark robes he seemed to glide backward across the other building. "But remember, do not jump.

Move. Believe. You are the power of yourself. You are one."

Remo took a few steps back to get up a running start until he saw Chiun's hand raise to stop him.

"I said, do not jump. I said move. Move your body. Move with your body. Look, beyond there over the ocean, dawn arises. That is your sun. You are becoming the sun source. See the sun. Run to the sun. I will never let you fall, neither will the sun or the universe."

Remo moved. His legs sank his body into the concrete railing, feeling it, knowing it, being one with it in the cool dawn, and he sensed the world, he tasted it on his tongue and on his whole being. The sun was rising before him, and his body was moving. When he landed he saw he was on the far side of the Master of Sinanju. He had jumped past Chiun, across the narrow alley between the buildings and over Chiun. He didn't even dare calculate how many feet it was, but it certainly would have been some sort of record, if he bothered to record it.

He smiled at Chiun. He had done it.

"Your elbows," said Chiun. "They were too wide."

"I would have set an Olympic record if someone were judging me."

"I was judging you. You failed," said Chiun.

"I'm not dead. I didn't fall. I jumped I don't know how many feet. Did you see what I did?"

"Most certainly. You let your elbows fly. I teach. And I teach and I teach. I give the best days of my life to you, and what do I get? Flying elbows. Now again."

Remo went back to the other roof, keeping the elbows in.

"All right?" said Remo.

"Of course, all right. I told you how to do it," said Chiun.

Remo was not certain when it happened, but he was sure one night when he woke up in a sweat.

"What is the matter?" said Chiun. Chiun was in the blue velvet sleeping kimono. He had tried to get Remo to wear a kimono but the young man didn't seem to be able to adjust to it, and besides, a kimono on a white might attract attention and that would violate the peculiar wishes of the black Con McCleary and his superior, Harold W. Smith, equally if not more insane.

"I couldn't remember my real name," said Remo. "I couldn't remember it. All I could hear about my name was that it was Remo because you were saying it was Remo."

"No," said Chiun. "You were saying it was Remo. Besides, who gave you your other name?"

"I think my parents. I never knew them. I was left at an orphanage. The nuns who raised me told me the name was pinned to my diaper."

"Ah," said Chiun in the darkness. "Discovery. I will tell you who your mother and father are, but you must be quiet within yourself to understand."

When Chiun could hear the silence of the large room, and knew there was silence within the young Remo, he spoke.

"Some say a mother and a father are those who give knowledge and love. Others say they are those who pass on life through their bodies to you. But I will tell you who must be your mother and father. For you as for all of us, it can only be one person."

"Me?" said Remo.

"Yes," said Chiun.

His name was Remo.

5

Harold W. Smith moved efficiently. He had always moved efficiently. In fact, he had been so excruciatingly reliable ever since childhood that one of his teachers once turned to him and asked if he could possibly act like a child for a day.

"In what way, ma'am?" asked the young Smith.

"Harold. Do I have to instruct you on how to be a child? Break a rule or something. At least mess your shirt like the other boys."

"Where do you want me to mess it?" asked Harold.

"I give up," said the teacher. "If you do it on my instructions, you are not being a boy. Do you understand, Harold?"

Harold Smith understood. Even in a New England town hardly noted for free expression, Harold was considered rigid. But he was not a fool. He would not drink until he was two years into the army because the law said he could not drink until age twenty-one. He honored stoplights at three A.M. at lonely intersections. How Harold Smith joined American intelligence services early in his life was somewhat of a mystery. Perhaps, as rarely happens, someone knew what they were doing, because Harold W. Smith had the sort of mind that could organize an avalanche. He saw order in all sorts of chaos. His rock-solid New England honesty enabled him to see things clearly. No reports were ever fudged for his advancement. This honesty would not let him, as happened to so many intelligence operatives, deceive himself. Thus when a now-dead President knew America needed an organization dangerously free of almost all controls, one man in the entire intelligence establishment stood out. Harold W. Smith.

The only one fit to run an organization outside the law was the one who had the most respect for the law.

As a result, admitting that the organization needed a killer arm was perhaps the most painful decision in Smith's career. And he was still not sure that reliable Con McCleary had not hung them all out on a limb. Smith had seen too many men killed at a mile's distance . . .blown up, shot, bombarded . . . to have faith in hand-to-hand combat, no matter what McCleary said. Yet they had to have it.

Smith glanced at the computer. There were still some problems with access to defense expenditures. Then he spotted the problem source. A computer at Grove Industries had blocked access to a military file. Regular auditing procedures by other agencies were being stalled. There was only one way to get past that kind of high-tech blockade: someone had to physically enter Grove offices, get access to their computers, and find the bug. Only then could Smith figure out how to remove it and let the government go about its business while making sure it wasn't robbed blind. Smith would send McCleary to do the job when McCleary had a free moment, which should be soon. Then Smith turned to the most important matter of the day. The new man.

McCleary had promised miracles. Smith by his nature did not believe in miracles. He believed in reality. But reality too was a very modern bullet that could not hit the Master of Sinanju. According to McCleary, the former policeman had fired at least three shots at Chiun at close range.

"Will Remo be able to do that?" Smith had asked.

"Speak to Chiun yourself," McCleary had said. He had said this with a smile. "But one thing. I want to be there when you two meet."

And so the day had come when Smith would see what America had bought with a submarine hold of gold. It was as though Smith was attending a parent-teacher conference for the new hired hand.

Chiun entered in a radiant gold kimono, ignoring all of the computers.

He's very old, thought Smith. McCleary entered behind Chiun, his smile becoming a grin. Smith had allocated fifteen minutes for the meeting. Ten minutes for McCleary to be late, and five minutes to get a summary of Remo's progress. Smith glanced down at his watch. The second hand arrived on the twelve at the minute the meeting was supposed to begin. And so did Chiun. But the man wore no wristwatch. His nails were long and graceful, the face parchment old, the hair but wisps of white.

It was five seconds past the moment scheduled for the meeting when Chiun's delicate fingers probed the air in greeting. It was a half-hour later when Chiun stopped glorifying Smith as an emperor, saluting Smith's power, divine right to rule, pledging the loyalty of the House of Sinanju to the glory of Smith's name and descendants. All the while McCleary's grin kept getting bigger.

"He thinks you hired him to place you on the throne. He doesn't understand what we do," said McCleary.

Chiun gave the whiskey-smelling servant a disdainful look.

"An assassin must understand an emperor's secret wishes as well as his proclaimed ones," said Chiun. "An emperor and his assassin never have servants in between."

"Yes, well," said Smith, clearing his throat and shooting a single sharp dirty look at McCleary's enjoyment. "I want to thank you for your services and we certainly are going to make use of your pupil. I would like to ask when you think he will be ready."

"With speed, with sureness, and with total dedication to your everlasting glory, Emperor Smith."

"I think I had better make this clear now. Master of Sinanju," said Smith, "I am not an emperor, nor do I wish to be."

"Of course, you are a loyal subject, but when you will be called upon after the most unfortunate death of the current emperor, you will serve as emperor as faithfully as you have served as subject," said Chiun and gave a knowing wink.

He sensed the machines around him, and saw the big American who smelled of alcohol and meat hold his sides to contain laughter. This did not bother Chiun. A fool's humor was meaningful only to another fool. Chiun could see clearly this Smith did not heed the whiskey drinker. A wise and sober emperor. Always good to work for. They made correct decisions, and left their empires in prosperity, thus bestowing further glory on the house of assassins that enabled their reigns to survive and thrive.

"Chiun," said Smith, "America is a democracy. We elect our leaders by voting. Every person over a certain age can vote. They select who will run the country. We have no emperors."

"As you say. Quite so," said Chiun. "What do you call the person you decide will run the country?"

"We call him President."

Chiun nodded. So that was the American word for emperor. Of course he could not quite believe something so absurd as people selecting their own leaders without an army at their back, but if Harold W. Smith whose gold was good said America chose its emperors that way and not by heredity or by the more reasonable and controlled methods of assassination, then Chiun would not argue. President it was. Democracy chose him, and Chiun was here only to serve. He would be ready when Chiun assisted Democracy in making him the new President.

"Hail President Smith," said Chiun. "We will soon remove the usurper from the President's throne."

"On second thought, call me emperor if you have to," said Smith. "When do you think Remo will be ready?"

"He progresses extraordinarily well. The question is how quickly can his body learn. After all, he has lived in such a bad environment for so long."

"In weeks, what are we talking about?"

"You want to know in weeks?" asked Chiun.

"Yes, weeks."

"All right," said Chiun, the longer fingernails working the air as though an invisible abacus lay before it. "If we use shortcuts, if we press the training, if his body performs as it seems to be performing, we can get you an assassin in a quick seven hundred weeks."

"That's fourteen years," said Smith.

"You said you wanted the time in weeks," said Chiun. He looked to the other barbarian. McCleary was rolling on the floor.

"What can we get in a month?"

"A month?" Chiun thought a moment. "Nothing you would want to carry your name to glory."

"Could we get a man for a job in a month?"

"I wouldn't if I were you. He shows promise. But a promise is not a deed. You could well kill him if you use him too early."

"A year?"

"Well, he has started late. A true assassin should begin at seven years of age. Still, he is a fast learner and I have given the best of Sinanju to his meager body."

"We'll double the gold payment if you can do it in a year," said McCleary. Smith shot him a dirty look.

"In a year, you will have your first head on the wall. The payment will be delivered by your undersea ships?"

Smith cleared his throat. "Yes." he said. He hated to waste money, and he knew McCleary knew it.

"Let me explain, we are a democracy, as I said. And our organization assists that democracy in working," said Smith. "We are secret. Therefore we need the natural kill. We need Remo to know how to do that so at crucial times, no one will know it is even a death."

"Of course," said Chiun. "Assist democracy." He had known it all along. Some future emperors were often hesitant about stating their goals, usually because their advancement involved the death of a parent.

An assassin had to know these things, be able to handle the delicate wording of them. A natural or accidental kill had made so many princes into kings. If Smith wanted, Chiun could even provide him, for modest extra cost, the most appropriate statements of grief he would most naturally make on hearing of the untimely death of the current emperor, in America called President.

"Yes," said Smith. "You understand. McCleary, you see he understands."

Chiun bowed. Smith nodded. McCleary wondered.

Smith got back to work immediately. The normal procedures to access certain government files were not working. It was that defense thing again. But now Smith was not only certain something was wrong, he was sure that it was wrong on purpose.

Private Anthony D'Amico pulled the trigger on the new AR-60 assault rifle, Grove Industries' latest offering for the defense of America. The AR-60 could shoot more accurately, faster, and under more difficult conditions than any other personal weapon in the history of warfare. That's what the specifications said. The specifications justified the fifteen-hundred-dollar price tag that went with each rifle. And the Army's estimate of how much it cost to train, feed, and transport a footsoldier justified the additional cost per unit. It all made so much sense, the Army had already ordered enough to equip a full division.

No one could deny its feasibility for combat. The gun was a miracle of design. The AR-60 field test was then just a formality. And of course to have a field test, one had to have a field. So the training center at Fort Baxter, Virginia, was chosen. And footsoldiers were chosen, and on this bright autumn day the squad marched to an open field in front of a reviewing stand and then as if in combat crawled forward across the field. Again, as if in combat, enemies appeared a thousand yards ahead of them. But unlike enemies these were all made of reinforced cardboard. And unlike most enemies they all exploded as rounds of AR-60 slugs poured into them. All of them, except the one Private Anthony D'Amico aimed at.

It remained unscathed. The man on his right had to mow it down. D'Amico was wincing in pain, holding his rifle limply in front of him. The sergeant came running over.

"D'Amico. What the hell's the matter with you?"

"The housing is loose. Touch the barrel. It's hot," said Private D'Amico.

"Screw the housing," snarled the sergeant under his breath. "Brass is on the reviewing stand. This is a show. Just shoot the damned thing. Don't feel it up."

"It jammed."

"Unjam it."

"It's the Grove AR-60."

"I know that. Just give it a bang, it will work. Now get moving. My squad is not going to foul up in front of brass, not Sergeant Johnson's squad."

Sergeant Johnson waved the squad forward. Few people on the reviewing stand had cause to notice what was going on between a sergeant and a private. Most of them had a master's in business administration in addition to their military educations. What one sergeant said to one private had little effect on the columns of numbers that symbolized modern defense to them. If one wanted to concern himself about battles and sergeants and privates, he was in the wrong mode for advancement. Unit cost, not flags and victories, was the way to stars.

But one officer did notice. Major Rayner Fleming focused on the private even while other eyes in the stand were focused on her full bosom and stunning good looks. She was used to that. She could have been a model, but being looked at was not exactly her idea of a career. She was Army, Army since her father raised her on a military post, Army since she graduated from West Point. And to her what went on between sergeants and privates was very important. Those were the people you fought wars with.

"What happened there?" she asked, pointing to the private holding his rifle a little bit farther in front of him than the others.

"Nothing," a colonel answered Major Fleming.

"I saw something. I think there may be a problem with that AR-60."

"I am sure the sergeant has taken care of it, Major. Beautiful day, isn't it?"

"Yes," she answered, knowing that the colonel was not staring at the day when he said that. "Both of them," she added.

"What?" asked the colonel.

"Nothing," answered Major Fleming. "They are going to rapid-fire now."

The squad fell to prone position on the far side of a ditch, and with a loud roar sent screams of lead slugs crashing into wood and paper targets of soldiers.

This time D'Amico's gun fired. It shot the housing back through his eye, throwing him with its force to the back of the ditch. D'Amico only remembered pulling the trigger and then watching the darkness of the universe close in around him.

In this last darkness, D'Amico thought he saw a single star, a very cold and small light in all eternity. And in communication far greater than words, it assured him that a force had been aroused that would avenge his death. But he didn't care about that anymore. He knew, like so many men just about to pass over into death, that he was no longer part of his body and there was a beautiful quiet about him. No more guns. No more pain. And for all time it would be this way.

Sergeant Johnson was cursing in the muddy field. He was cursing the gun. He was cursing himself. He was cursing the Grove AR-60 construction.

"We took the best of the batches and still they fouled, sir," he explained to the officers. But no explanation was necessary. The on-field explosion had triggered the distancing mechanism that had become second nature to the officers. Speaking in statistics and percentages, their backs to the field, they had all removed themselves from the problem, except for one. The woman. Major Rayner Fleming was now quiet, looking around the field. She picked up a piece of the barrel housing and saw the Grove label, and manufacturing number and plant number, on it.

She questioned the sergeant. She questioned the men.

"These were the best of the lot," Sergeant Johnson kept repeating as medics arrived to collect the body. They checked the pulse, they checked the heart, but they knew he was dead. The brain was already leaking out through the eye.

"So there have been problems with the AR-60?"

"Fucking useless, sir," said Sergeant Johnson. He was looking to the man he had just sent to his death. "Too many are just no good."

"Why didn't you report it?"

"We did, sir. I know for a fact the lieutenant and captain reported it."

Major Fleming questioned the lieutenant and captain.

"I am Major Rayner Fleming, of Weapons Analysis."

"Then why did you people, sir, okay this sort of demonstration, sir?" said the lieutenant.

"I am trying to find that out, lieutenant. Now let me see your report."

The report was of course in the limited-access computer mode, on the base. Everything the sergeant had said could be verified there. Major Fleming, using her clearance numbers, followed the report to her headquarters a few miles north to Washington, in the five-sided building known as the Pentagon. Her access did not read out.

"Minor problem," she said, taking the report numbers down with a pencil and paper. Funny, she thought. The last time I used paper and pencil was when I made out a grocery list.

She folded it in her pocket. She knew the Army. And she knew computers as well as any in the reviewing stand. She knew that when she got to her own terminal she would come at the report from the other end, and find out why exactly this unit at Baxter had been denied access to the overall weapons-performance chart.

But the next day, there was still that problem and an added one. An error in programming highly classified information on the major new missile defense system, HARP, had somehow resulted in data overlap. Reports on the lowly AR-60 that had killed the private the day before were now protected by the same computer classification that guarded the top-secret defense program. And she could not get access.

No one lower than a general could access HARP, and only a few of those.

Major Fleming smoothed her skirt just before she entered General Watson's office. General Watson's face was screwed in maximum concentration. He was taping the handle of his tennis racket.

General Watson had a suntanned face, immaculately combed white hair, and eyes of blue clarity seldom seen outside the Caribbean or a major gem. He was called the "old-style soldier"; that is, he believed in personal Washington contacts for advancement.

"Sir," said Major Fleming. "Some problem with the weapons-control computer access, sir."

"You know what I think of computers."

"For numbers, sir, they have been known to be more effective than the abacus."

"What's that, a new weapon? Don't flaunt your weapons knowledge at me, Major."

"No sir, an abacus is a Chinese counting device of beads, strung on wires."

"I don't follow the new China technology," said General Watson. He pressed the tape on the handle firmly against the butt. Good job, he thought.

"It's three thousand years old," said Major Fleming.

"No wonder it doesn't work," said General Watson.

Major Fleming hated these meetings. She once

heard someone say that "to know General Watson was to have faith in America's enemies, any enemies."

"Sir, I am being denied access to important information I have a right to have. We lost a man yesterday because of the AR-60 malfunction, and I have every reason to believe its problems are intrinsic."

"Then get rid of the intrinsic," said General Watson. "What the hell are you waiting for?"

She did not bother to explain that "intrinsic" meant a basic flaw within the Grove AR-60 itself. She was not here to make up for what his tenth-grade English teacher failed to do.

"I need you to help me access through HARP. For some reason there is an invalid overlay."

General Watson put down his tennis racket, mumbling something about war being hell. He personally supervised Fleming's access through HARP, and waited impatiently while she punched up the AR-60 reports, and the key-weapons-flow chart. And what they indicated was a persistent pattern of weapons failure, due to materials inferiority. Someone was shortchanging the Army, and so obviously that even General Watson could see it.

"I think we have a negligence case against Grove Industries, sir," said Major Fleming. And now General Watson showed where he had won his stars. He might never be too familiar with an order of battle, but he certainly knew where the important toes were.

"Negligence, Major. Do you know how many Grove plants there are? How many outside suppliers and contractors they employ? Any one of them could have been at fault. We could never prove negligence against Grove . . . even if we tried . . . believe me."

"Have you ever tried?" said Major Fleming.

"You made your point, Major. I'll see to it that it is included with the complete report I am making. Now if you will move away from the terminal, I will close access. We are in HARP now."

She saw the screen flash green, and then the program backed out of America's most sensitive new technology, the HARP.

"I would like to get field weapons out of that system so that I could get to it."

"Good idea," said General Watson, saluting. Then he turned and left, practicing his forehand through ordnance control, and marched right back to his office.

Major Fleming wrote out a report on the problems of AR-60 access, noting, with some emphasis, that all Grove AR-60 data as well as Grove HARP information was now protected by a computer system also devised by Grove Industries. Why, she wondered, did Grove seem to have its own special computer file, which obviously very few people could get at? In fact, if she were correct in her assumptions, just the people who should be getting into their files, could not.

6

Remo, alone at last in the safe house used for training, was hatching his own plans. When he saw Chiun leave with McCleary, he eased out of the door. It was amazing how quickly he moved now, though he could not imagine trusting any of this in combat. It might all be oriental mental tricks. But this day, he had a plan he had been working on secretly for weeks. It was crucial that he not fail.

Once on the street, he joined moving crowds as though one of them, careful not to move too quickly, careful to appear just like anyone out for a little stroll. He did not want to give anything away. He paused, waiting to sense if Chiun were around. There was no sense of the man. The Master was gone. Remo crossed the street. As he neared the far side, he couldn't stop himself. He broke into a run, almost tripping a group of young men. He dodged a patrolman lounging against a lamppost, almost knocking the man into the concrete sidewalk. Remo didn't care. Let the guy try to collar him. He was too close. He could smell it.

Up ahead something was broiling. It filled his nostrils, and his senses. He dashed through the crowds at the doorway, moved up to the front of the line despite angry stares, and blurted:

"Make it two quarter-pound burgers. Plenty of onions."

Remo Williams had gotten to a hamburger.

Afterward he went into a druggist's and asked a question that left the man confused.

"Do you have anything that can remove hamburger from the breath?"

Someone suggested whiskey. They were joking. Remo was not. It took him a large part of the afternoon to find something. He only hoped it worked. Certainly it tasted bitter enough to be effective.

When he eased back into the main training room, he tried not to cast his breath too far forward. He heard a strange noise. Chiun was gasping.

"No," said Chiun.

There was another voice in the room. It was a man's voice.

"I'm sorry, Jim. I've got to level with you. That leg's got to come off."

Who was Jim? What leg?

"No, I was going to be an all-American." This from a young man. Remo was still in the doorway. He couldn't see into the room. He took one more step, a gliding move that shifted the weight before the feet, not using the feet as normal people did to pull their bodies along with clumps along the ground, but to move the body itself.

There in a glaring red flowered kimono sat Chiun, transfixed before a television set. Remo had never seen Chiun direct himself so totally at any one thing. You were supposed to remain balanced internally at all times so that you would not be surprised. He felt he could pounce on Chiun now and the old man would not be aware. On the other hand, if he were less than fully aware he might kill Remo without knowing it at this point.

A man in white on the television screen answered the young boy.

"You can be an all-American for courage," said the actor who was supposed to be a surgeon.

"Does Mom know?" answered the boy.

Then Remo realized: Chiun, who thought nothing in this barbaric country was worth a notice, had been transfixed by the simple soap opera *Love and Death.*

"That," said Remo, "is a soap opera."

"Shhhhh," said Chiun, turning slowly. For the first time, Remo saw anger in the eyes of the Master of Sinanju.

"Jim's mother doesn't know," said Chiun, going back to the screen.

When the commercials came on, Chiun turned off the television.

"You were watching a soap opera, Master of Sinanju," said Remo.

"Your country's one undeniable contribution to the arts. It concerns family, love, honor and courage . . . all that is noblest in the human spirit."

"That's a soap opera," said Remo.

"You never told me they were on every day," said Chiun. And then quite coldly, he said: "Out. Out with it."

"With what?" asked Remo.

"The meat. You ate meat. You went out while I was gone briefly. And you put meat into your system."

"That was an hour ago. It's digested."

"Not yet, meat reeker. You ate cow meat. You

couldn't overcome your roots. You couldn't rise above that den of ignorance where you were raised. You put dead cow meat into your belly, the belly I trained, to feed the body I trained."

"I was hungry."

"You had a half-inch of fat around your thighs. I have seen on your television all the problems you people have losing weight. If they used the fat for energy, which is its purpose, energy stored like a barn stores grain, then there would be no fat problem. You had fat on your body which you did not need. Then why did you add more dead animal to your system? Think about that, while I change."

To watch Chiun change was to be deprived of the opportunity to think about anything else. The Master of Sinanju had all the natural desire to expose his flesh to air of a cloistered nun. Somehow the robe Chiun was wearing was levitated above his head while from underneath it came its replacement. Only when the new robe was securely on, through some miraculous form of body contortion Remo was sure, did the one he was originally wearing come off. And then it was with utmost discretion and modesty. His new evening robe was pigeon's-egg blue with embroidered depictions of Chinese palaces and swans swimming before them. Remo had seen it once before. The colors, Remo thought, would have embarrassed a pimp.

"Do you have an answer yet as to why, when there was no reason to, you added animal meat to a body that had fat? A body I trained?" said Chiun.

Remo shrugged.

"I was hungry," he said.

"You were hungry. I have given you the greatest secrets of all mankind, and you were . . . were . . ."

"Hungry," said Remo. He had a right to eat. He had gone along with all this but he had not given up his right to eat. "Yeah, hungry. Do you mind?"

"Of course I mind," said Chiun. "Give you Sinanju, and prepare you ultimately to be an assassin, and you put dead cows in your mouth because that was the way your mother and father taught you." The wisps of hair quivered.

"I didn't have a mother and father."

"Really, then to what do I attribute your existence? One of your American machines in Detroit?"

"I mean I didn't know my parents. I was dropped off at an orphanage, and I was raised by nuns."

"And they taught you to put this filth into your body?"

"Actually, we didn't have much meat."

"Yes, nuns are your virtuous women, yes? I know about nuns. We know your white customs. You had vestal virgins and then you had nuns later."

"I didn't have any vestal virgins. I don't know of any vestal virgins."

"The Romans," said Chiun. "They had them just seventeen hundred years ago. Romans. You whites."

"Well, I'm not Italian," said Remo.

"You don't know what you are," said Chiun. "You're an orphan, you said. Whoever got you first ruined you. They trained you to murder your senses by filling your belly with dead cow meat."

"No special training. We just eat meat. We are meat eaters. I am. I like a glass of beer and a hamburger from time to time," said Remo. "I like to rest. I like to just not think about breathing. I like to just live."

"They should have buried alive those nuns who let you do such things. They lacked strictness."

"They were very strict," said Remo.

"White?"

"Most of them."

"Hah," said Chiun and then turned to the forces of the universe, his eyes heavenward to bemoan in front of Remo what had been cast before him. "I try to give him the sun source of all human power, I try to raise him to be an assassin, and what do I get? What is my reward?"

"I am not going to feel guilty," said Remo. He kicked the wood floor of the training room.

"I didn't ask for guilt," said Chiun, righteously folding the robe around himself.

"Well, you're not getting it. I am doing damn well. And I do not believe, excuse me please, I really do not believe that killers and murderers are so elevated in the world that a bite of a hot dog will ruin them morally. Yes." Remo stuck out his chin on the last word.

Chiun was quiet. "I suppose I deserve this. I suppose I have failed."

"You didn't fail."

"Not for you to say, yak dropping," said Chiun. "I will tell you how I failed. I will tell you how Sinanju has failed in its one way throughout the ages, especially me."

"What do you mean? You've been telling 'em about this emperor or this prince or that general that dies instantly under your hands no matter how they protect themselves. When I am not breathing in new ways or jumping across buildings, I am hearing about how to approach someone when he is guarded by one, by two, by a wall, by this and that and the other thing."

"Our problem in Sinanju," said Chiun, ignoring what Remo had said. "If we have one problem, it is that we are too nice."

"You're the deadliest killers of all time."

"I deserved that," said Chiun. He folded his hands under his kimono.

"Aren't you?" said Remo.

"We are not," said Chiun.

"Then what are you?"

"We are," said Chiun, "assassins. Something I think you never will be."

"An assassin's a killer."

"A swan is a bird. A sunset is a reddish color. The sea is water."

"Well, is there something more? Am I missing something?" asked Remo. Chiun looked at him a moment. Remo had learned to breathe in many ways. The bulky plodding fat had melted off his body. And he did listen at times.

But then again, after seeing the gleam of the star in Remo's soul, Chiun had given him so much. Why shouldn't he have been so far along?

And then he went out and put meat into that body Chiun had given the best to.

Chiun moved to a steamer trunk where one of the training devices was. It was something that would be most familiar to this white, something he had used himself.

It was a pistol with six bullets in it. Chiun did not like the feel of guns. Their very power robbed the true power of mankind. But it was a fitting tool for a meat eater. Chiun aimed the pistol at Remo's chest and fired twice.

* * *

Major Rayner Fleming did not have to attend the special funeral mass for Private Anthony D'Amico. She did not belong to his division. She didn't know him personally. Major Fleming went there to collect the tears, to bring back something to remember if she should ever falter in the face of all the red tape and bureaucracy or if she should ever be tempted to listen to General Watson's reminders about what was good and bad for her career.

And in the little town of Wilton, Pennsylvania, she got the memory she wanted. Anthony D'Amico's grandfather, who could barely speak English, came over to her after the funeral mass.

The old man had been in the Italian Army in World War I. He knew an officer when he saw one.

"I talk to you, officer, even though you are a woman. Please do not take this as offense," said the old man. "Tony, he was my favorite. I love that boy. I love him still. My heart will go into that grave. But I say to you. This is a good country. This is a good Army. It fights for good things. So there is no war now. I know my Tony die for this country, just as if someone, he be shooting at us. Do you understand?"

Major Fleming nodded.

"He die so that our boys, they no go into war without good guns. We had bad guns sometimes in Italy. But in America, our boys, they have the best. Just the best."

"Sir?" said Fleming.

The old man looked up to her.

"Yes, sir," said Major Fleming. She had everything she needed. She was ready to do battle with General Watson, commander of the deadly flanking memo, power behind the committee, daring leader of the newspaper leak, and defender of the bastion of Congress.

The good general might not know a cannon from a Cuisinart, but he knew the voting pattern of every congressional district in the country, and could find a way to get a part of a weapon built in every one of them. And Major Fleming was ready to take him on in his own chosen battleground, the five-sided Pentagon.

General Watson easily disposed of her first complaint with a full report, enveloping any criticism in four hundred pages of technical language. The brilliance of this maneuver was not lost on Fleming. Should anything continue to go wrong, there was General Watson's report with the warning included. But he had as neatly turned both its flanks with technological reports on the projected efficacy of the AR-60, and at the last minute committed the entire Navy to its use. He had won the day. There was no use fighting against the use of the Grove AR-60.

What Fleming had to do was make sure Grove delivered AR-60s that worked, or pay the price. It was strictly rearguard action. Somebody had to make Grove accountable. She leaked a story on how the AR-60 might let America down in a war.

But to her amazement, there was General Watson on television calling the AR-60 "the gun of the future, for the soldier of the future."

"But, General, we hear that they are badly made." This from a television reporter.

"We are always open to any reports you might have. The one thing we value, and work for, and continue to work for, is reliability. And we welcome any reports anyone might have of guns not working. Do you know which one didn't work?"

"We heard there was an accident with one, that a soldier was killed."

And then General Watson's clear blue eyes stared into the television camera, a face that exuded integrity of the highest order.

"That would be one in a million. One in a million ain't bad."

General Watson had won again.

But he did not have time to feel pleased with himself.

"Meet me at the tennis club," came the voice.

"I have an important staff meeting."

"You have a more important one with me."

"I can't do it," said General Watson.

"I don't like that word. I don't believe that word. I did not hear that word. Scott, if I really heard the word 'can't' I would believe that word. Then I would believe I couldn't do things either, Scott. Do you understand me?"

Within a half-hour, General Scott Watson was changing into his tennis whites at the club. So was George S. Grove, chairman of Grove Industries.

They had adjacent lockers.

"Saw you on television yesterday, Scott. You looked good."

"What do you want, George?"

"I don't want to see you on television. I don't want to see people talking about Grove equipment as having flaws. We are headed for the biggest, absolutely the biggest defense venture in the history of this nation, and I don't want some stinking little rifle to ruin it."

"George. We lost a man with one of your rifles."

"So?"

"The soldier was killed."

"Well, sweet Jesus, Scott, soldiers are supposed

to be killed. What do you think they give out medals for? Give him a medal. Have a parade, but, Scott, don't hold television news conferences."

George Grove was a middle-aged man with hard dark eyes. A smooth face and hair graying at the temples gave him a benign appearance. That face exuding benign strength appeared on more fund-raising brochures than the symbolic open palm. George Grove helped the needy, and he wanted everyone to know it. In public he called giving "the only right thing to do, when you live in the best and strongest country in the world." In private he called it part of the whole program. The program included more than just public giving. It was the private gifts that made you the real friends you needed.

One of those friends was Scott Watson, now General Watson. Grove had known him since he was a captain.

"You don't understand the military, George," General Watson complained.

"I understand it will do us no good to have bad things said about our products. I understand that," said Grove.

"You just don't kill a report. I handled it rather well."

"Then why did I see you on television?"

"Because someone leaked a story."

"And what are you going to do about it? What you should've done before this little issue made you a star?"

General Watson laced his sneakers.

"Scott," said George Grove. "Uncle Sam gave you your uniform. I gave you everything else. You will take care of it."

"Tennis, George?" said General Watson.

"No," said George Grove. He had work to do.

"Somebody has got to tell you who the leak is in your organization."

Grove Industries' Washington headquarters was in an elegant Georgetown mansion surrounded by what many considered the most beautiful gardens in the capital. Quiet and elegant discreet meeting rooms, overlooking lawns and trees and flowering shrubs.

But inside, one could not overlook the power Grove Industries produced. There were models of special shells that could wipe out companies. Sensors that could track a mouse at five miles. There were automatic weapons and computer weapons. Sketches of them, paintings of them, sculptures of them.

Everything in Grove Industries told the visitor that without Grove, man was helpless. It was the triumph of the tool over the user. All soldiers were interchangeable—only the weapons were different. George Grove designed the displays himself. He knew what made people work. He also knew how to make the weapons to make them not work, forever. And he was well aware of how his building made him work. It reminded him what fun it was to control the deeper thoughts of his people, the Pentagon's people, and the world's people.

George Grove walked through seven electronic checks hidden in pictures and ornate doorways until he reached his office.

"Wilson. I want Wilson," he said. No one was in the room. He lowered himself to the soft leather seat behind the glistening mahogany desk. He drummed his fingers. He ignored the models of weapons. They were not for his benefit, or even for Wilson's. They were for visitors.

"Wilson," he said into a small desk speaker.

Wilson usually did not take this long. Finally an elegant man in his mid-forties, hair perfectly combed in a traditional part, his two-thousand-dollar dark pinstriped suit looking as though it had been steamed off a British prime minister, entered the office. His name was Jim Wilson. The man was always so immaculately dressed, George Grove at first believed he might have been homosexual. But the awesome competence of the Grove Industries background check proved this not to be so. In no case had Wilson ever had to anyone's knowledge a liaison with another male.

Nor did he have liaisons with females. Finally, Grove was forced to ask him what in hell he did for kicks.

"I buy things," Wilson had answered. "Expensive things."

In that one moment, George Grove had found a man whose purpose was to be bought for money. George Grove had found a man he could trust.

"These generals. Pin a few stars to the shoulders and they become impossible."

"You have a problem, Mr. Grove?"

"No, I called you because I want a look at a well-fitting suit. Wilson, we have the most important defense project of our entire corporate history moving through Congress, moving well and expensively I might add . . . given enough to charities to feed the poor fifteen times over . . . cure diseases they haven't even invented yet . . . supported enough Boy Scout troops to make a second army . . ."

"Mr. Grove, the problem."

"General Scott Watson has got a leak in his staff. If he doesn't know what to do, you do."

Wilson nodded.

"The leak isn't the only thing that worries me. We have problems closer to home. Who is this?"

Grove flipped several eight-by-ten glossy photographs onto his desk. Wilson picked them up. They were of a black man, conservatively dressed in a cashmere jacket and striped tie.

"Yes, I remember him. Just yesterday. He had perfect identification from the Internal Revenue."

"Really. Then why did these photographs appear on my desk this morning?"

"Well, there was a problem. His fingerprints didn't jibe with any in the national directory of anyone working in a sensitive government post."

"That should be impossible," said Grove.

"It should be, but from time to time we run into many impossibles. They happen."

"Only when someone makes them happen."

"If there is a someone, we have no inkling. And if we don't know, no one does. Perhaps I shouldn't have lumped all the problems together."

"No, there are too many accidents that somehow help the government. I can live with the fact that sometimes, for no apparent reason, a congressman who is bought, gets unbought. Some law-enforcement official we own suddenly does his job. Not just against us. It happens to others, more and more. But sometimes, Wilson, even you swear there is some ghost out there with central access to government files, a ghost screwing things up for us."

"Ghost was just a term I used for a whole bunch of computer phenomena," said Wilson.

Grove ignored the explanation. He pointed to the pictures of the black man.

"Wilson, I want to know who he is and who he works for."

"Mr. Grove, sooner or later, our sources always

prove to be greater than anyone else's. We'll find him."

"Well, I don't like it. I don't like things I can't control. That's how you get destroyed, not controlling things. And what the hell is he grinning about?"

"I think he saw the camera in the ceiling, Mr. Grove. I imagine he is some sort of a wise guy," said Wilson, who did not know that Con McCleary was always up for these little jokes: they broke the monotony of living in constant terror.

7

The beautiful part about being a defense industry was that Grove Industries had an absolute right to be protected by the government. And Wilson knew the government, though not as well as Mr. Grove. Mr. Grove was a benefactor of political powers, military men. Of every dollar spent by Grove to make America safe, thirty-seven cents of it was spent on making sure America kept on letting Grove Industries keep it safe.

Wilson's special expertise was in two fields. Use of government protection, and when that failed, other things. One never mentioned the "other things" but considering that government protection meant anything from undercover agents to gunship helicopters to defend the secrecy of military projects, rarely were the "other things" needed.

This was fortunate for Wilson, because the "field personnel" who were most adept at the other things made Wilson's delicate stomach turn. He was not a man who loved violence. It was just that arms manufacturing was where the money was, and Wilson knew how to use money, lots of it.

Therefore Grove Industries was both mother and father for all his needs.

He wasted no time bringing the picture of the intruder at Grove headquarters to the FBI building and his main contact, an agent named Harmon.

The first thing Harmon asked, even before he studied the picture, was:

"He didn't get access to HARP, did he?"

"No," said Wilson.

"Did he try to get access to HARP? We have to know. The Air Force would have to know. The Joint Chiefs, I think, might have to know."

"No, he did not get access to the HARP system," said Wilson. Harmon was a ruggedly handsome man with a neat gray suit. But Wilson saw it did not mold to his shoulders and the stitching around the lapels was pure off-the-rack. He wondered if Agent Harmon or people like him actually were aware of the stitching on the lapels. He thought not. All the FBI required was a tie and neatness.

"Was the HARP system accessible to the computer he entered?"

"The HARP system was."

"Damn," said Harmon. He had a small office with one window. It overlooked an adjacent building. It was not what Wilson would call a power office. Especially not with the dull metal desk with the gray top. The carpeting could not have been more than ten dollars a yard, suitable for an even lower government functionary. But Agent Harmon was one of those who probably never even wondered what the pile depth beneath his feet was. He was, however, a conscientious worker. If not, Wilson would have asked George Grove to get the Justice Department to give Grove another man.

"As you know, we have more safety precautions surrounding the HARP system than any other project in the nation's history. That is a major part of our operating budget," said Wilson.

"I don't even admit this to my wife, Wilson," said Agent Harmon. "But it terrifies me how much we are going to depend on HARP in the coming years. And the Joint Chiefs are probably five times as concerned as I am because they know what is going on."

"No one gets into the HARP system," said Wilson. "The security systems we have for HARP makes Fort Knox look like a vacant shed, and the first atomic bomb an advertisement on prime-time TV. It is the most advanced security system in history."

"Glad to hear it," said Harmon, shaking his head. "But it gives me the willies that some guy off the street can get into your computers at all."

"What the intruder accessed was some form of finance control concerning a personnel weapon, a new rifle, the AR-60. Why he got no further, incidentally, was that there is an A-root access code, what our computer people tell me is a sub-path to information, shared by HARP. Everything turned off, and the cameras started shooting away. But apparently this man was a professional agent of some sort because he knew enough to get out of there right away."

"The Russians?" asked Harmon.

Wilson shrugged. "His voice and manner were American. That couldn't be disguised."

"Russians use Americans. They use Bulgarians, Czechs, too," said Harmon.

"I don't have any idea where this one comes from," said Wilson.

"Well, if he is American, and if he is a professional, maybe he is one of ours?" asked the FBI inspector.

Access to a defense computer was a nightmare to counterintelligence operatives. In an age of technological warfare, the spies and those who chased them were not people who skulked through alleys, but those who understood the effects between RAM chip and atmospheric pressure on missile parabolas.

The very plan of battle for war was not in some general's head, but in what a weapons system could do or hope to do. America's vulnerability was inside the memory of defense-company computers.

To allow unauthorized personnel to break into those systems, especially Grove Industries' file now that it was working on HARP, the last, best defense hope of the near future, was to take off the protective roof from every American home. And like missing roofs from America's homes, people would realize it most in a rainstorm. A nuclear rain.

Harmon felt himself hating that smooth black face in the picture. Who could be arrogant enough to smile at a surveillance camera? To Inspector Ralph Harmon, this man was laughing at his country's safety.

"His prints don't check with our own security files," said Wilson. "And you know our fingerprint files are almost as good as yours."

"Do you have them?"

"We got the right hand. The left gave us no impression," said Wilson. "The prints are on the back of the photographs. We can give you separate copies if you want. We thought one piece of paper was always better than two. I distrust paper."

"Do you think this man might have anything to do with your leaks on the AR-60?" asked Harmon.

Beautiful, thought Wilson. "I don't know," he said.

"Now, we are not in the business of stopping people talking to the newspapers. And frankly the technology of a field weapon is not going to endanger us a whit," said Harmon. "Dammit, the enemy is going to capture three or four hundred the first time they ever see action anyhow. Or maybe before, from warehouses some punks break into. The reason I ask about the leak is only because of HARP."

"I just don't know."

"We'll look into it, but frankly, your sources in the news media are better than ours."

"We try," said Wilson.

"I'll bet," said Harmon. He only suspected Grove power, but he knew it had to be enormous.

"And maybe we succeed a bit," said Wilson modestly.

"I saw something on the AR-60 the other night. A general was defending it. He made a good case. I only hope the gun is as good as he says it is," said Harmon.

"It is," said Wilson. "It might be the best rifle we have ever built. But when someone, somewhere, questions whether a gun is functional, doubt is cast over a whole program. One simple slip of the lip, and one million guns are put in doubt. And then it becomes an attack against the morale of troops. All that damage is done with the first words."

Wilson had every confidence in Harmon. He was a good man. Grove Industries liked to use patriots. They were better than the people you had to buy. You could always trust them to do their jobs.

* * *

Inspector Harmon made copies of the pictures of the smiling well-dressed black man and circulated them throughout the intelligence agencies. He sent them to key FBI offices. He did not know he was also sending them to a computer room in a bank, where only one man ever seemed to go to the twentieth floor during working hours, a New Englander who took his hat off in the elevator and was never known to start a conversation. Everyone in the building thought of Mr. Smith, who brought his lunch every day in a brown paper bag, as an actuarial analyst with a very large private practice.

This day, the computer itself interrupted Smith's work with a flag. A flag was a form of alarm. It flashed a small red light to indicate there was something Smith should look into. If it were important enough, it would break into anything Smith was working on. First came the small red light in the upper corner of his screen, and then, everything else disappeared. Thrown onto the screen was an alarm that something might compromise the secrecy of the organization. It was a confirmed image of McCleary and his fingerprinting confirmation on the right hand.

The FBI was looking for him and the prints. Smith watched the electronic memos route themselves throughout the government. The prints even went into the CIA files because the FBI suspected this man might be a former government agent. Good guess, thought Smith. But there, where they had once been, they no longer were. Smith had had them removed years before when he had chosen this man despite obvious personal flaws concerning drink and women. The thing about Con McCleary that made him so worthwhile was that he got things done. And he was loyal to his country.

What McCleary had done most recently was to raid the AR-60 files and verify what Smith had suspected: they had used the secrecy of the HARP system, namely its multitudes of electronic defenses, to shield all their operations at Grove.

McCleary had found the parameters of the blocks by trying to get into HARP, and then all Smith had to do was send them back into the Grove system, and let the Grove teckies (technologists) think they were repairing an access problem. They would simply show Smith how to get in without ever knowing they were doing it. Then Smith would make access to the AR-60 available to the proper Army sections or the General Accounting Office that made sure Americans got what they paid for.

Smith waited as the warning filled the screen with information as to who was looking for what and how much they knew. Looking in on this world, safe from detection but able to influence events, was almost like playing God, he thought. And as soon as the thought became conscious, he pushed it from his mind.

The good Lord was always sure of what he was doing. Smith only hoped he knew. He didn't try to stop the search for McCleary. That would only create an information block and as soon as someone discovered the wall was there, they would figure out how to scale it, break it, or get around it some other way.

So one did not block, one redirected. Smith sent in a security clearance for McCleary with McCleary's face and prints, under the name Mel

Bergman, computer engineer, Grove Industries, Grove, Idaho, on special assignment Taiwan.

Then he created a payroll record for Mr. Bergman, including complaints about withholding. He created a system for Mr. Bergman that would enable Grove and the FBI to chase him for months, and then declare him missing.

This job finished, Smith phoned McCleary.

"I'd like to see you in the shop," he said. He had reached McCleary's apartment.

"Does it have to be now?" asked McCleary.

"Yes," said Smith.

Smith heard a woman's groan through the receiver.

"Does it have to be now? I have met the one woman who stands me on end. I have never in my life been so moved. And I have never met someone who is so intelligent, and kind and courageous, weak when she should be weak, and strong when she should be strong."

"Will it be long?"

"As long as I can make it."

"Well, make it quick," said Smith. "I don't suppose you could be here in a half-hour?"

"Something important?"

"I think we might be in danger. Nothing firm yet. Something I want to talk to you about."

"I'll be right over."

"What about your woman?"

"I'll return her to the bar I met her in twenty minutes ago," said McCleary.

There was a scream of indignation on the other end, but McCleary was at the "shop" within twenty minutes.

"What's wrong?" he asked.

"Grove Industries," said Smith.

"I got what you wanted right on those little

floppy disks you had designed so that they could pass through security and not be destroyed."

"I didn't design them. The CIA designed them. Con, how many penetrations have you done?"

"For work?"

"Yes, work," said Smith, realizing he should have let McCleary finish what he was doing with the woman. It would be on his mind all day.

"A hundred. A hundred and twenty. It's not really something difficult with all the really valid identification you can get for me."

"And how many did you have to flee from because they saw through what was going on?"

"Two," said McCleary.

"And how many were able to mount a search for you right within the United States government itself?"

"None," said McCleary.

"One," said Smith.

"Grove?"

"Yes."

"Well, that only shows how well protected they are from spies. We should like that in a defense industry."

"Except when they seem to defend themselves too well. They got to the CIA, McCleary. That's closer to you than anyone has gotten before."

"Anyone remember me?"

"No, you were a small Far East branch. I made sure all of those who knew you by face, sound and walk stayed in the Far East."

"Those were the only friends I had."

"Those were your drinking buddies. You didn't have any friends," said Smith.

"I know," said McCleary. "But when it comes to these things, you should be allowing a man to lie to himself."

Smith understood the loneliness of it very well. This man, who would have preferred to spend a life pleasantly over a beer in a bar, chose instead to defend his country. McCleary, unlike Smith, was the sort who did need friends. He just didn't happen to have accumulated any since high school.

"I'm worried," said Smith.

He wore his three-piece gray suit and sat on a stiff-backed chair before a computer terminal. McCleary wore an open shirt showing a gold chain on a hairy chest, and loose gray pants. He lounged against a computer storage unit.

"You think they are going to come after us?" asked McCleary.

"I think we might be needing the new man sooner than we expected. With Grove we sent in General Accounting. We sent in Army comptrollers. We even isolated a major in the Pentagon and fed her enough information to get her on the case. But nothing has worked so far. The only one able to get into Grove Industries' books is Grove Industries. I've never seen anything like it."

"What about me? I got in."

"You were our last resort. And now they may be coming after us. What is the situation with Remo?"

McCleary shook his head. "I don't know. I think there might be some trouble there."

"What's wrong?"

"Nothing's wrong. That's what's wrong. Every day until two days ago, I heard one complaint per twenty-four-hour period from Chiun about Remo. Every day. Now nothing."

"Which means?"

"I don't know. Maybe the training was too hard. This isn't karate Remo is getting. It's not a martial art. It's Sinanju. These bastards run across thirty-story buildings. These assassins have survived three thousand years because they are not too tolerant of mistakes."

"What are you saying?"

"I'm saying that if a Master of Sinanju ever failed, he felt his entire village would starve. So the training is not designed to give someone a colored belt. If it succeeds, the man knows Sinanju. But if it fails, well, another failure and you go on to the next candidate. It's life and death from the very beginning."

"You think Remo may be dead."

"I haven't heard a complaint from Chiun for the last two days."

"Well, maybe you ought to find out."

"Yeah," said McCleary. "Except you don't just call up a Master of Sinanju and ask if he's killed the pupil you stood on your head to get for him."

"What do you do?"

"You wait until he phones with another complaint."

"Call him," said Smith.

The Master of Sinanju was approached in an extraordinary manner at a most unfortunate time. The Lawsons' son, Jim, had survived the operation, only to find out that while he couldn't play football anymore as an all-American, he did have a fantastic talent as an interior designer. Yet to become an interior designer meant endangering his love affair with Jill Anderson, who had escaped Mafia threats to become the only addict of a special drug meant originally to cure her grandfather's rare case of leukemia.

It was, of course, the grandest art form of the west, a surprising respite from the drone of this civilization. It was the one meager pleasure Chiun allowed himself.

And the phone call came before the advertisements for the washing products.

Chiun, of course, did not answer it, and made sure its ringing would stop. He wondered why the Americans did not stop all telephones while this art was in progress. Of course great art, like great assassins, was not always appreciated.

On the other end Con McCleary heard the phone go dead.

He cursed under his breath. He wondered whether he should take a gun. He probably wouldn't be much better than Remo with a gun. Therefore, a gun would be useless.

Throughout the far reaches of Asia, legends of the Sinanju assassins maintained that the Masters never failed. To McCleary's mind, this meant that no one lived to tell of their failures. Maybe they protected the reputation of Sinanju by burying their mistakes, six feet under. Maybe an emperor they failed never woke up some morning.

Would it be important enough for them to kill a client? McCleary thought about that. Of course it would. What else did a centuries-old house of assassins have but its reputation? How did he hear of them? The legends of perfection.

Remo was a bit of a wise-ass. Maybe he made one wise-guy remark too many.

Con McCleary thought about these things as he drove to the training house on the West Side, the large barn of an industrial building with a brownstone façade. He found a parking spot immediately, and he was disappointed. He would happily have driven around another hour looking for a spot. It would have meant another hour of breathing.

"Time to find out what's what, laddie," McCleary told himself in a voice so clear it might have been to another passenger. But the words he did not mouth were, "Time to die."

At least it would be quick if it happened. The Masters of Sinanju did not waste time with cruelty. They were too perfect for that. They might lead people to believe they were cruel, but only to reinforce the legend in people's minds.

That was the most important lesson one Master had taught to Ivan the Terrible, the especially brutal Russian czar. And that was one of the references that had convinced Smitty to try Sinanju.

In the early years of Czar Ivan's reign, a French noble recorded in his diary that the czar told him of a magnificent house of assassins that could do anything. By the time the name reached the French language it was Seinajuif. But the location was clear. This was the village on the West Korea Bay, and what the noble recorded in French was that Czar Ivan had said:

"These Masters understand things we will never know. Things we blunder through, they dance through. They even understand the wildest acts and what they mean. For example, they say that the place for cruelty is not on the victim, because the victim will ultimately be dead. In that case it serves no purpose at all. Where it matters is in the minds of others. It matters that the living think you will be cruel. But cruelty, they say, is a wasted stroke, an imperfect move. An unnecessary thing."

Thus the quote secondhand that McCleary reminded himself of as he entered the training house. The simple translation was that he was going to die quick if he were going to die.

He entered the brownstone and climbed up a flight of steps.

The door opened as though it had never been on a hinge. Chiun stood there, the bright day from the skylight filling the whole room. He wore a green kimono with flowers.

"Hello," said McCleary.

Chiun did not answer.

"I called before."

Chiun still did not answer.

"I bring greetings from Smith . . . Emperor Smith. . . . He sends you greetings."

Chiun nodded.

"May I come in?"

"There is more you have to say?"

"Yes. More."

"And it was so important that you carelessly sent messages to me at the most inopportune time?" Chiun's squeaky voice quivered with rage.

McCleary looked for Remo. There was no sign of him. Was that blood at the far end of the room? Or was it an old stain? McCleary couldn't tell.

Chiun stepped back, beckoning McCleary to enter. McCleary stepped into the room leaving the door open behind him. Chiun pointed an imperious long fingernail at the rubble of what once had been a telephone.

"Fix that," said Chiun.

"We'll get you another," said McCleary. Where was Remo? The door shut. He looked behind him. No one was there. Could Chiun will a door shut? McCleary glanced up to the high rafters near the skylights. Where was Remo? He focused on the smells of the training room. Dust. No lingering odor of a death. Even more strange, where was the smell of sweat? Didn't these people sweat? If there was no sweat, there was no exercise.

McCleary noticed Chiun was just staring at him. Saying nothing.

"We will get you another," said McCleary.

"I don't want another," said Chiun. "I want it fixed. Another will be broken. Fix it so that it does not ring during your daytime dramas."

"He means soap operas," boomed Remo's voice. It came from a place behind McCleary.

McCleary turned around. Remo wasn't there.

"Remo?"

McCleary heard Remo's chuckle.

"Did you teach him to disappear?" McCleary asked Chiun.

"Can you do that with the phones?" asked Chiun.

"Yeah. Sure sure. We'll get a television schedule and we'll do it. Glad to do it. Done. We'll do it. Where's Remo?"

"Playing," said Chiun.

McCleary felt a slap at the back of his head. He turned, swinging a fist. There was nothing there. Another slap. Another swing, and on the last swing he saw, in the farthest peripheral vision of his leading eye, gray slacks.

"Eeeah, failure," said Chiun. "You move like a pregnant yak. Your pig feet stumble across the floor. He saw you. You lost concentration."

"He didn't see me," said Remo, now standing quite casually within McCleary's vision.

"You were inside the room right behind me all the time and you moved with me," said McCleary.

"Nah," said Remo. "I was outside and saw you park the car, and followed you up the steps. You walked like you were afraid. Were you afraid?

Sometimes I can't tell. I try to tell. Chiun says you can tell. I don't know."

"A little," said McCleary. "So everything is going all right."

"All right?" asked Chiun. He gave a little sarcastic laugh. Chiun turned from both of them. Sadly, he walked into the other room, and McCleary could see him opening one of the many steamer trunks.

"You were great, Remo. I didn't know you were there at all. I didn't suspect it," said McCleary.

"Not that good. Not that good a test."

"What do you mean? I'm an old CIA hand from Southeast Asia. I am one of the best tests in the world. You were just a cop."

Remo shook his head. "You were afraid. If you're afraid, you don't see as well, or hear as well. Fear fills your senses. Like ask someone to walk across a two-inch line on the floor. No problem. Put it fifty stories up and they can hardly move their feet. They could never stay up there. Fear. You don't hear as well, sense as well."

"Fear gets you going, adrenaline," said McCleary.

"Maybe for running or swinging a rock, but anything else, forget it. I know. Me it will kill," said Remo.

"What are you talking about?" asked McCleary.

"I can't explain it. The way I am learning, and what I am learning, it's not muscles. It's breathing. It's the mind."

"I don't understand."

"Wait a second," said Remo. Chiun was coming back into the room.

He carried a pistol. He took the pistol and brought it up no more than five feet from Remo's chest, aimed it at Remo and fired twice. The barrel flashed an ugly blue-yellow.

Two cracking reports rattled McCleary's eardrums. He blinked and shook his head. There was Remo. No wounds, nothing.

"Shit," said Remo.

"Yes, excrement," said Chiun.

"Blanks," said McCleary.

Remo shook his head. "Blanks won't do. Blanks are training. Blanks are training for blanks. Look at the wall."

Behind Remo white plaster dust was still misting from the wall. They were real bullets and at five feet away, they couldn't have been misaimed. Remo had dodged them. He could dodge bullets.

"Sweet Jeeee . . . That's awesome," said McCleary.

"The two, yeah. I have two. Two I have," said Remo. There was consternation in his voice.

"Yes," said Chiun. "Two he has. Two he has and with two he remains," said Chiun. All Remo could ever get to was two bullets in a row. Chiun never fired the third because it would kill him. And the why was obvious to any thinking person. "Remo prefers to chew the dead flesh of animals than to allow himself to be what he should be. What he knows he should be. What I have told him he should be . . . Me. Not that he will ever be me. But he should at least try, after all."

"I had a hamburger," Remo explained.

"Sinanju lays before him golden pearls of the wisdom of the grandest house of assassins in all history, and he must feed on the dead. Animal. Are you a wolf? Are you a dog? A cat? A rodent?"

"A big-deal hamburger," said Remo.

"I think Chiun is saying that perhaps the methods he teaches you are so refined," said McCleary, "that even a hamburger can harm your performance."

"You don't know what I say," said Chiun. "Ask him why he ate the hamburger; then you will find the infamy behind it all. Ask him. Go ahead."

"Not again," said Remo.

"Ask him," said Chiun.

"Here we go," said Remo. He turned away from Chiun, his shoulders slumping. For McCleary it was like looking at a teenager.

"Go ahead. He'll tell you," said Chiun. He folded his arms, in the true indignation of one whose sufferings were now going to receive their righteous airing. Perfidy now readied itself for its ugly exposure. "Go ahead. Ask."

McCleary shifted his weight. He felt uncomfortable. More important, he was sure that either man could kill him now. He didn't want to get in between these two.

He cleared his throat. "Say, Remo. I am doing this because I am asked, and I feel I have to. Why, if I may ask, did you eat the hamburger?"

Chiun nodded in delicious satisfaction.

"Because," said Remo, "I was hungry and it tasted good."

"Ahah," said Chiun. "You see. Out of his mouth. His own words. There we have it. Do we ever have it. Have it right there. This, McCleary, is what you bring me to train. This is what I am supposed to work with."

"Excuse me, Master of Sinanju, but I am a bit perplexed. Aren't those the reasons people eat?"

"There is a whole race of them here," said Chiun. "You too."

"Don't push this one," said Remo to McCleary.

"Of course, don't push it," said Chiun. "Then

we will have answers. Then we will have truth. As for hunger, that is your stomach talking. It does not know your body as well as I do. Your body, Remo, is the product of some sexual accident followed by almost thirty years of abuse. It is hardly the wisdom of Sinanju."

"I have not taken to living off my fat," said Remo.

"It will be gone soon if you do not interrupt the process again. You are not so skilled in movement that you must handicap yourself with extra weight."

McCleary said nothing. Remo looked in rock-hard shape to him.

"But even worse, he eats because something tastes good. Does he ask himself, 'Will this food assist my nervous system in responding to the magnificent teachings of the Master of Sinanju?' No. What does he ask himself? 'How will my tongue react?' His tongue. He has me here to guide him and he listens to his tongue and his stomach. I would hate to hear how he chooses a woman. I venture it is not for the quality of the offspring you might produce."

"You venture your ass right," said Remo.

"He is even proud of it," said Chiun.

"It looks pretty good to me," said McCleary. "He dodged, actually dodged two bullets."

"That's right. That is wonderful," said Remo. "That's great. That is effing great. Great. I am wonderful. Hey. I'm wonderful."

McCleary did not see the blow but he knew Chiun had delivered one because as the smooth ruffle of the green kimono passed Remo, Remo fell as though collapsed by a wall coming down on him. He did not move. Even his muscles did not twitch. He was deathly still.

"Is he . . .?"

"Dead? No," said Chiun. "He is asleep. Come to the far side of the room where the animal fat clogging his ears will prevent his unconscious mind from hearing us."

McCleary followed the shuffling figure. Chiun paused a moment, and McCleary could tell he was waiting for attention.

"You want him as your assassin for whatever your reasons."

"Yes," said McCleary.

"You see things that look wondrous to you."

"They are amazing. You have far exceeded our greatest expectations."

Chiun shook his head. "You see things you cannot do, and you believe they are wonderful. In a small way, yes. They are wonderful to you. But these things you see are not Sinanju. They are not Remo's."

"I don't understand," said McCleary.

"When you hear about something, does that mean you can do it?"

"Of course not," said McCleary.

"If you can describe something, does it mean you own it?"

"No."

"If you hear of something or describe something, still you have nothing. Yet these are the first steps toward having something. What you see are the tender shoots of bamboo, not yet a tree. It may look to you like a tree but you cannot build with it. Remo knows enough to do things when I am with him, near him, providing the power for him. But without me near him, his mind may wander and the tricks you see will no longer be his. They are not part of him yet."

"What you're telling me is that we should extend your contract so you will be with him. Is that right?" said McCleary, recognizing an old Asian bargaining ploy when he saw one.

"No," said Chiun. "I am telling you that if you use him now, use him too soon, as I most certainly sense you wish to do because you rush everything . . . you will have nothing."

"What do you mean?"

"You will kill him," said Chiun, and turned his back on Remo's countryman.

8

George Grove had an interesting way of making sure people felt as deeply about things as he did—he yelled at them. He also fired them, promised big bonuses, and paid well, but from threats to promotions, all personnel matters were settled at ninety decibels or above.

Every management consultant who ever worked for Grove Industries, however briefly, reported that this was "an archaic and counterproductive personnel policy." And Grove fired them on the spot. Often when he yelled he would spit. His secretary, an elderly woman named Mrs. Marker, was amazed at how many personnel consultants could pretend there was no spittle on their faces and walk out smiling. The consultants called what happened in Mr. Grove's office "divergent policies."

Grove called it spitting in their faces. Sometimes Mr. Grove slapped. But he never slapped Mrs. Marker. She was sixty years old, one of the last remaining examples of old-time efficiency, and she was married. She would walk out if he raised his voice to her. For her Grove made an exception—he needed her.

Mr. Grove did not slap people to hurt them, she knew. That was not his pleasure. His pleasure was seeing how much he could humiliate them and still keep them. He had once told her it was like fishing with a light line. You tried to land the heaviest fish with the lightest line possible. His goal was to be able to slap any worker in the face, then let him apologize for it. Only then was George Grove sure he had someone. He called those incidents "trophies."

Mrs. Marker called "trophies" revolting.

"I never want to be in the same room when you do that to someone," she said.

"I am experimenting with human nature. America's defense needs it. If you can't deal productively with America's defense then maybe this is not the right place for you."

"Mr. Grove. You've tried that before. You can't replace me. I know what a good English sentence is. They don't make that kind anymore."

George Grove would laugh at that. But it was true. When George Grove really wanted to get something done, he stopped playing games with personnel. He became as unemotional as one of his machines. At times like that, Mrs. Marker was indispensable. This was one of those times.

For a week now, Grove had yet to humiliate anyone. He was too busy, burning up the lines on the special scrambler phones to Wilson five times a day. Wilson, after Mr. Grove himself, was the highest-paid employee of the entire vast network of Grove Industries. Only he had access to the vast sums of unaccountable company cash. Only he had immediate access by untappable line to Mr. Grove. And only Wilson made Mrs. Marker's skin crawl. Wilson's eerie lack of feeling for any human being under any circumstances made George Grove's sadism look like a spiritual gift. Wilson had been in Mr. Grove's office during an especially vicious humiliation. The secretary knew that grave damage had been done as soon as the top executives began to file out of the room ashen-faced. One of them asked openly, "How much are our inflated salaries worth?" Another bore a glaring red handprint on his cheek.

Wilson had walked out of Grove's office nibbling on a doughnut.

"What happened in there?" asked Mrs. Marker.

"In where?"

"Mr. Grove's office. Who was humiliated?"

Wilson flicked a hint of a possible crumb off his dark blue designer suit.

"Oh, I don't know. George was at it again. It's his hobby. I think he likes to upset an audience. I wish I could get upset. It would make George happy. But I don't," Wilson had said, and then his face suddenly tightened in a frown. It made his very smooth skin look like a collapsed leather bag.

"Is that a Bonwit Teller suit?" he asked.

"As a matter of fact, it is," Mrs. Marker had said.

"I thought so. Good lines."

"I guess I should be grateful that you didn't tell me what happened in there."

"I honestly didn't notice. Their suits don't fit, you know. Executives getting paid six figures a year, and none of the suits really fit. Do you know what I mean? Really fit," Wilson had said.

But for the last week, in the two times he had come back to the main office, not once had he commented on clothes. And if it were not Wilson, she would have sworn a collar button might have been missing.

Now Wilson was on the phone again, but this time he wanted Mrs. Marker.

"Has Mr. Grove seen the personnel report?"

"He's been looking at nothing else all week," said Mrs. Marker.

"And what does he think?"

"Wouldn't he tell you if he wanted you to know?"

"He would if he weren't so busy. I am working at a similar problem from another end. Tell him I might have the answer tomorrow."

"Very good," said Mrs. Marker and buzzed Mr. Grove.

"Mr. Grove," she said. "Wilson says he will have the answer to your problem tomorrow. Possibly."

"The hell he will," answered Grove. "I have it today."

"Do you want me to tell him?"

"No. I want to tell him."

"Very good, Mr. Grove," said Mrs. Marker.

The problem of course was the leak to the media. Who had informed the press about the AR-60? Wilson had a working knowledge of weapons and a superior knowledge of finances. He knew that while it might cost a quarter of a million dollars to stem a leak, to retool an entire factory could cost tens of millions. Therefore, one did not foolishly spend ten million dollars on retooling and investing in higher-grade steel when one could simply put in a plug.

So a soldier was killed. Soldiers were always getting killed. If several thousand had been killed, then that of course would call for a change in the factory itself. But until then, it was absurd for

Grove Industries to go running around changing manufacturing policy, when all Wilson had to do was take the Grove jet up to Boston to meet a friend, a columnist who ironically was against the defense establishment, anything to do with American power, and usually anything favorable about an American ally.

But this columnist worked on the same New York paper that had first reported problems with the AR-60. What Wilson wanted to know was who had informed the press. And to do that he had to know which reporter got the tip, and to find that reporter, he had to ply his Boston source. He did not fly with an envelope of cash, or with a gift of an interest-free mortgage, or even with a promise of influence or promotion. Nor would he use blackmail or an extremely friendly woman adept in his special brand of press relations.

Robert Tarbush was not someone who could be bought for ordinary things. What one paid to Robert Tarbush was far more subtle.

Robert Tarbush was a columnist of international reputation who, from his elegant Boston town house, wrote three thunderous columns a week, rubbing readers' noses in what was wrong with America.

Robert Tarbush waged moral campaigns around the inequities in the world. He found these inequities only in America's allies. He pointed out oppressions, until these countries were officially "liberated" by communist forces. Then he would turn to other "oppressed" nations allied to America. One could always tell when Robert Tarbush thought a nation no longer needed his moral watchdogging. One could always tell when one of those countries had been liberated. Their freedom began when their new communist government started to shoot people at the border for trying to escape.

Wilson's coin for buying Tarbush was simply to let him know how good a new American weapon was. Then Tarbush could reveal the weapon, the newest "enemy of humanity," to his readers. Tarbush believed that this employee of an arms manufacturer, the man with only one name, Wilson, believed as he did, secretly. This Wilson accomplished by simply nodding once every minute, and interjecting every so often a sincere "how awful, too awful for words."

It did not matter really that Tarbush attacked Grove weapons. Only the people who believed like Tarbush ever read him. And that was very few. But Robert Tarbush never knew that. He never spoke to anyone who didn't believe as he did, nor did he leave his Boston home.

Tarbush was therefore at home, deeply engrossed in a television program, when Wilson entered.

It was a dramatization of a work of fiction about India. The drama was very good. The novelist had added his artistic interpretations to what happencd in India during the Second World War, and the screenwriter added his to the script. Then the director added his own to the shooting of the film, so that by the time it was ready for showing, it had no more to do with the reality of India than a cartoon. The difference was that a cartoon never claimed to be truth.

Wilson had to wait through this program so he watched patiently while a British official, upon hearing of the atomic bomb drop on Hiroshima, was stunned by the absolute horror of it all. Somehow, six million people stuffed in ovens hadn't offended him, nor did the Japanese rape of

Nanking. To this British official, the bombing of European cities, which killed many more people than America's Hiroshima attack, was not a horror. Nor did the bleeding of Britain's populace during its bloodiest war seem to bother the queen's own man in India.

"And I suppose this will be the end of the war," the British official said on the television screen, reaching for a file folder. Tarbush was nodding at the wisdom of the broadcast. Once again, the only real horror of the war was perpetrated by the Americans, who also managed to end it.

"And we won't know the true horror of Hiroshima for twenty years. Terrible business. Horrible. But a magnificent show," said Tarbush. Wilson nodded.

"I will write that everyone should watch it. Then they will know what is happening in Nicaragua."

"Good idea, Bob."

"They will see how wrong we are, and how wrong we've been since World War Two."

"How true, Bob."

"This is as close as you'll come to seeing the truth on television, you know." Tarbush gestured toward the television set, now airing live coverage of a gruesomely unsuccessful public broadcasting fund-raiser. "You'll never get the truth from the network news, that's for sure. Really, the things they allow news reports to show."

"Awful. Just awful. And I'm afraid I've come to talk about another awful thing."

"What has America done wrong again?"

"Well, Bob," Wilson said to the columnist who was adjusting himself in his easy chair. If Tarbush didn't move in his chair, Wilson knew, the doctor warned he would get skin lesions from sitting there so long. "We have a problem. Someone with a distorted world view is getting things into your newspaper."

"They do that all the time; they embarrass me. I like to think Boston is above that sort of thing."

"Well I think someone in the military or our own industry is helping them."

"I hear from people who visit that those kind are all over. Though where they are exactly, I don't know. I am always shocked when decent humanitarian candidates are defeated. Do you know anyone who votes against them?" asked Tarbush. He did not wait for an answer. "Neither do I."

"I need the name of your reporter, and the name of the person who gave him that information. Your reporter did not use a byline, but his story was picked up by the networks. Then, of course, the entire nation saw it."

"That's what I was saying before—that's how lies get started. And then those who don't know the facts, who don't know the people we know, will go right out and believe all those lies just because they're backed up by a picture on the television screen."

"So you know why I need your help," said Wilson.

"Of course. You want to find out who is spreading those lies. At least now we can do something about it."

"I most certainly will," said Wilson.

Within fifteen minutes, Wilson had his answer—the reporter was a cub on the military beat.

The last thing Tarbush said to Wilson before Tarbush began his column on the state of the world was:

"Why are you wearing a coat?"

"It's winter, Robert," said Wilson.

"Already? Wasn't it spring last month?"

The reporter was a tougher nut. He not only wouldn't divulge his source, but asked Wilson why he was so interested in the leak. What was wrong with Grove Industries that it should be so concerned? Wilson dismissed the questions. There was nothing wrong with Grove Industries, but considering what Grove meant to America's defense, Grove had to be concerned with any leak, no matter how harmless or ill-founded. Undaunted, Wilson tried the reporter's city editor but he couldn't reach him either.

George Grove himself called off that operation, though Wilson wanted to continue. He was sure he could work something out with someone at the newspaper, but if worse came to worst, he could use the "other means" Mr. Grove did not like to discuss. Wilson's reasons were simple and strong:

"HARP is coming up. Congress is holding hearings on further development. If AR-60 becomes a bigger scandal, then it might spill over to HARP. And the last thing we want is anyone looking into HARP."

"And killing a newspaperman might be the fastest way to attract unnecessary attention," said Grove. He was robust this morning in his vast office with the high Georgian windows overlooking the Grove gardens on the Georgetown estate. "Wilson, I know men. More important, I know our people. I have tested them. I have tested their limits. I have looked over a list of everyone who might know about the AR-60 and have narrowed it down to five people.

"Of those five, one has made phone calls to that paper. Very cleverly too. He first asked for the advertising department, for Classified. Then he hung up."

"I don't understand."

"When he hung up, somehow his real message began. He works in accounting. His name is Nathan Archer."

"Do you want me to get all the details on how he delivered the message? We might be able to use it in the future."

"Of course," said Grove. It was a good day. There was no way they wouldn't get all the details, and very soon, from Mr. Archer. Wilson, of course, was about to use the "other means."

Nathan Archer felt dizzy after his first cup of coffee at the Grove headquarters cafeteria.

"I don't know what I ate," he said. He stood around for a few minutes trying to keep his balance. Then he had to sit down. If he were working at any other company but Grove, he might have been in trouble. But Grove Industries had their own medical facilities near every plant or major office. Some were as small as clinics. Others, as in the Washington headquarters, were lush hospitals.

Nathan Archer got a private room. By evening he was feeling absolutely fine.

"Feeling fine? You haven't felt nearly enough," said the doctor.

What did he mean by that? Archer didn't want to waste time asking.

"But I am ready to go," Archer said. "My wife is worried."

"We'll decide when you're ready to go, Mr. Archer."

"You can't keep me here," said Archer.

"Then just one test," said the doctor. He had incredibly blue eyes and hair so blond it was almost white. A diamond glistened in his front tooth. Nathan Archer never remembered seeing a doctor with a diamond in his tooth.

"Last one?"

"Promise," said the doctor with the ice-blue eyes.

He helped Nathan buckle straps to his legs and wrists. Then he attached small electrodes to Nathan's scrotum. Then he shot electrical currents into that most sensitive part of the body.

"Does that hurt?"

Nathan could not answer. He was screaming, but no sounds came out. He was screaming into a reinforced gag. The ice-blue eyes smiled.

"Does this hurt?"

Nathan Archer almost tore his arms out of their sockets trying to leap from the bed.

"Now, we can either ask that question or we can ask another question."

Nathan tried to speak with his eyes. He tried to say, "Other. Other." The gag was still in place.

"All right," said the man very pleasantly. Back to question number one. "Does this hurt?"

When the face was red, contorted in pain, and when the body continued to tremble after the electricity had been turned off, the gag was removed.

"Other," sobbed Nathan Archer in a voice that was barely a whisper.

"Good," said the man in the white jacket. "Now why did you phone the New York newspaper?"

"I was selling a house I own in Westchester."

"Good, and after you spoke with the Classified

department whom did you speak to? More important, what did you tell him?"

"I didn't speak to anyone."

The pain began again. Nathan Archer did not understand the questions that followed, like how he managed to deliver the message after he hung up and what the new device was. He stayed in the hospital all that night, and in the morning he was dead.

Wilson approached George Grove with the bad news.

"Archer died this morning," said Wilson.

"Okay, what's the bad news?" asked Grove.

"He wasn't the leaker. Someone else is working against us."

"Are you sure it wasn't Archer?"

"Stone did the questioning," said Wilson. "Stone had him in one of our hospitals. He had him in straps. He had him all night."

"Someone is working against us," said Grove. He was quiet a moment. "What about that phony IRS man who got into our computer system briefly?"

"We got the FBI report this morning," said Wilson. "They found that the man who belonged to that face and those fingerprints was a Grove employee named Mel Bergman."

"Maybe he's the leak," said Grove.

"No. It was a very cute trick. Somehow these people have access to the FBI computers, and what they did was to plant a phony name. Oh, there is a real Mel Bergman but he wasn't the man who visited the plant that day."

Wilson paused. He hated to admit one of George Grove's hunches was right. He hated business by instinct. The multiple accidental problems were now obviously not so accidental after all.

"In creating somebody for us to chase around the world forever, these people have finally given themselves away."

"I knew it in my gut, Wilson. There are no accidents in this world," said Grove.

"And I suspect they know all the tricks we do, George. You don't try to misdirect unless you're hiding something. And what are they hiding?"

"Who they are," said Grove.

"Exactly, George," said Wilson.

"Well, it is a bit discomforting to find out you have an enemy, but there are always the good points. Once you know you have an enemy, you can destroy him."

"Exactly, George. As for the leak. It might be whoever planted their version of Mel Bergman. Or it might even be someone on General Watson's staff as we thought earlier."

"The trouble with trying to get General Watson to act is the man is terrified if he doesn't have some damn committee behind him," said Grove. "I have to kick him every step of the way."

"You were wrong about Nathan Archer in accounting," said Wilson.

"I said of all the people we had, he was most likely responsible for the leak. I did not say he was the leaker. Finding out he was not the leaker tells us we don't have one."

"Yes, George."

"Get the other bastards."

"Yes, George."

"Are you just yessing me, Wilson?"

"No, George."

"You are," said Grove. He loved being right. When Wilson was gone, he put a small mark on his calendar. It was the date by which he was sure Wilson would find their new enemies and remove them quite successfully from the face of the earth. Wilson did not miss.

9

Chiun saw the way Remo moved. He saw the legs and the torso. He saw the head. He even saw his pupil's will to move forward. And there was a great choice to be made here this day by a Master of Sinanju.

He let Remo climb the obstacle course in the room, chairs on their sides, brooms to be balanced on, the unsure footing where a man had to sustain the balance he achieved by proper breathing.

It was this harmony that made Sinanju. Some men, even sons of some Masters of Sinanju, never achieved a glimmer of it. There was no shame of course to the family, just a funeral. When one lost his balance on the heights one lost his life.

There was a saying in Sinanju that one should never love a child training to be a Master until manhood, when it was assured he would live a long time.

"Off the broom to the chair," Chiun said. He watched the bristles touching the floor as Remo jackknifed his body off it onto a chair, without pressing the bristles too hard. His movement had that wonderful look of effortlessness, the look of purity. Was it in this man? That glimmer he had seen of that far-off star in this white's eye . . . was he seeing it in the performance of the body?

There were many stages in a person's life, and the difference between a Master of Sinanju and the normal person was that the untrained never knew when one stage began and another ended. The crossroads of their lives were only apparent in memory. The great power of the Masters of Sinanju was they could perceive these stages as they happened.

This white man with this white name was at the threshold of a new life. Should training proceed, and if he were properly trained—which of course could not be a question with Chiun—this white man without mother and father would become Sinanju. Not for years would this happen, of course. This was not some silly little instant teaching from the west where they called people trained at thirty. At thirty a man began to grope with his skills. At forty he began to suspect what he did not know, and only in the latter fifties did real skill begin to show.

Chiun had gotten this one late. Who knew how long it would take? Right now, he still had that problem with heights. He could be killed. And then where would Chiun's training be? Remo would be dead, and Chiun would have wasted the best of Sinanju.

And then of course there were the problems with the crazies. The entire nation, most of all Smith, was mad. True, Smith had delivered the gold properly, so there was some intelligence there. But the claim that his fondest hopes were that his nation would live safely under a form of government stolen from the Greeks, and that he had no personal ambitions himself, was not something the mature mind could take seriously.

So what were Smith's plans? Why did he want one of his own to be a personal assassin? Smith might be just like the cunning pharaoh of the fourth dynasty in Egypt, who had attempted to swindle Master Toksa and Sinanju. That too had been a training mission, so very rare in all history. The underhanded plan was for the pharaoh's nephew to become Sinanju, destroy the priests of Karnak vying to control the Nile, and then eliminate the Master of Sinanju, saving the treasury the rightful tribute to Sinanju.

That plan was easily foiled by showing the young man how to eliminate his uncle, but when the youngster assumed his divine office of pharaoh, he too refused payment, saying he had not been fully made Sinanju.

Master Toksa explained to the pharaoh that no one outside Sinanju could ever be Sinanju but that the pharaoh would always have the services of Sinanju.

"I was promised to be trained. You did not train me."

"I trained, lord of the Upper and Lower Nile, master of Thebes, son of Ra, blessings upon this sacred presence. You received training. You were never promised to be Sinanju. But you were given the throne. That is the best an assassin of Sinanju can give."

Master Toksa did not mention, of course, that there were many kings in the world—every spit and jottle of a country had one—but there was only one Master of Sinanju. The secret to dealing with emperors was to let them continue to believe how important they were. And in their own limited lands all of them were.

But this pharaoh, twelve years of age, lacked judgment.

"Here I am lord. And I decree what is fair payment. When you make me as good as you are, then I will pay you."

"O great pharaoh, lord of the Upper and Lower Nile, master of Thebes, son of Ra, blessings upon your sacred presence, we of Sinanju are a poor village. We live by the services of the Masters of Sinanju. If the pharaoh decrees a change of payment, such is your fame that lesser lords will attempt to do the same and then kings and satraps and chieftains will withhold payment also. And we cannot afford that."

"Is this a threat I hear, yellow-skinned of the slanted eyes?"

Many in the court of the pharaoh laughed. It sounded strange, Master Toksa would record, because their heads were pressed to the polished floor.

"Sinanju does not threaten, O lord of the Upper and Lower Nile, son of Ra, whose sacred presence blesses us all."

"Some misjudge me because I am twelve in age," said the pharaoh. "I know your powers. But they are useless. The only purpose to kill a pharaoh is to replace him with another. But you do not have another. And of course no yellow-skinned can be a real ruler. One must have the skin colored of the mud of the Nile."

The pharaoh chuckled. The court laughed.

"Admit it, you of the funny eyes. I have outwitted you."

Master Toksa rose from his formal bow.

"You will not see thirteen," said the Master.

"I thought you never threatened."

"I don't," said Master Toksa and he walked directly to the throne, snapping the chest bones of the two foolish guards with fast enough reflexes to slow him down, and cracked the young skull of the pharaoh.

Then the Master of Sinanju laughed, and then the court was silent. There was no pharaoh in the land of the Upper and Lower Nile.

But that was not the business of Master Toksa.

Of course, no one could allow it to be known that a pharaoh had been dispatched with the ease one might use to crush a grape. In Egypt there was little trouble in hiding it, however, since the people always knew the priests and the pharaohs were struggling for power. Pharaohs as well as priests died suddenly without the populace being any the wiser.

And of course, another pharaoh was found equally divine, for the truth was, there is always another emperor, but only one Master of Sinanju.

Only when the pharaoh's mummy was discovered by Englishmen, in the western century numbered nineteen, did they find out that Tutankhamen had been killed by a blow to the head.

These things were well remembered in the dirty air of the great city of the barbarian called New York. And as Chiun remembered this, and thought about Smith, and thought about Smith's strange orders, Remo went through the proper lessons before Chiun's exacting eyes.

Remo was moving in harmony from the chair to a stacked box, to a tilted table and then back to the broom. He had learned far more than Chiun ever expected. To continue was to move him along the road to something Master Toksa could never give Tutankhamen, Sinanju itself.

Remo alighted from the broom.

"It felt right," said Remo.

"Hmmm," said Chiun.

"What are you thinking? You seem to be thinking something. I didn't sense that you were with me."

"I think you listen too much to compliments from fools."

"You mean McCleary, the other day. It impressed him."

Chiun placed a delicate fingernail under the wisp of white beard.

"Tell me, Remo, as we eat, about yourself."

"I am going to eat?"

"The fat is gone," said Chiun.

Remo felt around his body. The skin was taut. "You're right."

"You have moved into another stage."

"I didn't notice it until now."

"That is because I show you and the stage is passed."

Remo didn't understand what Chiun meant by that. He was too busy thinking about food. Even the rice Chiun had promised would be good.

"I will be back with the food before you can say 'Jack Robinson,' " said Remo.

Chiun was puzzled about this. Why would he want to say "Jack Robinson"? It wouldn't help him find out if Remo had any plans to become some sort of emperor nor would it help Chiun ex-plain that what Remo could have was far beyond what any common king might aspire to. Remo might become a true assassin.

Remo did not find the kind of rice Chiun wanted in the grocery and he was referred to a health-food store on the Lower East Side. As night settled, New Yorkers disappeared from the streets, leaving them to the muggers, and occasional policemen trying to stay alive.

Perhaps it was the training. Perhaps Remo's desire to eat took away his awareness, but three tall black men, their hair hanging in dreadlocks, got close to Remo before he noticed they were there.

They had been following him for blocks and now they had the jump, all three pushing him into an alley. They smelled as though they never took baths, just reapplied mud to their heads every day. But Remo was not bothered by the odor.

One of them had a knife to Remo's throat.

"Okay, man," another said in the sweet singsong of the islands. "Reach for your wallet nice and slow."

The man with the knife was even friendlier.

"I don't want to cut you, white boy," he said.

Remo felt his shirt being ripped open. A hand played around his neck. They were looking for a chain.

Don't panic. If you panic you can't do anything, Remo told himself. But he was too light to fight his old way. He was too skinny to butt and bang and hit. And then he knew he was panicked. One of them yanked at his wrist. They got his new wristwatch, the one he had bought despite Chiun's admonition against relying on time.

"Shit, it's a cheapy," said one of them.

A garbage-can lid came banging against the wall right next to Remo's head.

"You come here to score some smack, pretty boy?"

Remo didn't answer. The third assailant had a chain that swished viciously in the air.

"Come on, man. Give us the cash."

Remo pulled one hand free and reached into his pocket, giving them the first thing he felt. It was a dollar. It was rice money, his meal money.

One of the blacks looked at the dollar in the dim light.

"Hey, man. That not funny. What you gonna buy wif a dollar?"

"Rice."

"Hey, his old lady send him out for rice," said one.

"And he get lost," said another.

Remo did not know what happened at that moment. Perhaps his mind, seized in fear, had wandered. Perhaps he thought about Chiun. Perhaps he had noticed a star in the sky, but suddenly he was breathing, and more important, the breathing was happening. He was, at that moment, everything he was supposed to be.

The three muggers did not notice that muscles no longer strained against their grip.

"Actually, an old man sent me out for rice. Busts my ass all day working my fingers to the bone."

Remo penetrated the trashcan cover with a finger. Then he put three more holes in it, very loud. Life rifle shots. He felt the hands release him.

"I climb walls a lot. Jump off buildings. You know that kind of stuff."

Remo grabbed the chain from the black man and spun it around. Then he held it in front of the three. Then he snapped it in two.

One of the men suddenly felt his bladder give and urine ran down his pants leg.

"You know how I did that? Breathing. That's the most important thing. Lots of people don't realize that," said Remo.

The man with the garbage-can lid suddenly realized he had a very important meeting at that very moment at the other end of Manhattan in Harlem. Since cabs were so negligent about picking up blacks at this hour, he decided to get there by running. And he left the garbage-can cover with the three holes in it because it would have slowed him down.

Also wanting to make this late-night rendezvous in Harlem was the man whose bladder had decided that this was not the right time to hold in bodily liquid wastes. He took off admonishing, "Feets, do yo thing."

The accent of the islands was gone.

Only the man with the knife was left, and he had a very strong impulse to see that no one was hurt. Suddenly he felt a compulsion to explain to the white man, to establish a great bond of communication with him.

"I close it now, man. Slow. See . . . now I put it away."

He slipped the knife into his pocket and smiled, holding up his hands in a gesture of peace and friendship. Then he backed out of the alley, laughing with the good-natured white man, knowing that this evening brotherhood had triumphed over a simple mugging. They were all friends after all. And when he reached the street, he gave a last warm smile, then ran for his life.

"See ya," said Remo.

It had all worked. And it had worked under pressure. Remo bought his rice, and couldn't wait to tell Chiun.

"You know that thing where you taught me to put holes in a fingerboard? I did it under pressure."

But Chiun did not seem impressed. He did not even seem to care. He took the rice to a small wood stove he had insisted be built in the corner two days before.

There he boiled water.

"Remo, you know this man Smith?"

"I met him once," said Remo, watching every grain in the bag.

"What are his plans to be emperor? How do you fit in them? Does he want you to rule after him?"

"What?" asked Remo.

"Does he want you to rule?"

"Rule what?"

"The country."

"No. What are you talking about?"

"Smith appears like a fool, but he is devious."

"I think he is a bastard. I met him once, which means I have no great desire to meet him again, but no, I don't think he's devious. I just don't think he has any feelings. Coldest bastard I ever met."

"Yes, but why does he talk about things secret unless he plans devious things."

"Well you see, we are a democracy. And we live under laws. But under the laws the country isn't working . . ."

"I give you Sinanju and you return this wondrous gift with lies."

"It's true."

"Worse," said Chiun. "You believe them."

The rice was not ready soon enough, and further delayed because Remo had to be taught to eat. The teeth were for grinding, not for talking. The rice should be ground soft in the mouth, not liquidy, and never be swallowed in chunks.

"You know, it's no fun anymore. I am just eating to stay alive," said Remo.

"You learn well for a white," said Chiun.

"I guess this . . . this . . . gruel keeps you alive a long time. How old are you, really? I mean, you are old, Chiun."

Chiun ate his rice properly. Later, when the student learned more, he would be allowed duck. Honey when his inner tone resonated with his body. But now rice was right.

"For an apricot, yes," said Chiun. "I am old. For a head of lettuce, I am even older. But for a mountain, I am not even begun in years. For a man, however, I am just right."

"Yeah, well, now I know," said Remo. "Ever been married?"

"Yes. She bore me a son."

"Yeah? Where is he?"

"He is no more," said Chiun. Some survived the training of Sinanju and some did not. Chiun did not mention that he had lost the boy because he had failed to conquer heights one day on a Korean cliff. Nor did the Master reveal how he loved the boy despite the old admonitions against doing so until fully trained.

"It is better to follow the admonitions," said Chiun, "than to learn them on your own. There is less pain."

At that moment, though he did not know why, Remo felt sorry for the old man who had never shown him any form of concern.

"What about sex?" said Remo.

"When you are ready to make a child, then you will do it."

"I'm ready now. I have been ready every day, and I'm getting readier every day that passes by. I am more than ready. I am ready to explode."

"Then we will teach you soon how to do it. There are many steps leading to the end of your explosion—thirty-six to be exact—and twenty to bring the woman to perfect sexual bliss. Actually, seven usually gives them bliss. Women like bliss."

"Go ahead. I'm listening," said Remo.

"The left wrist locates the woman's pulse with the middle finger and, tapping in time with the pulse . . ." Chiun paused, pondering the rice in his mouth.

"Yeah. Then what?" asked Remo.

"Then we cook the rice longer," said Chiun.

"The sex. What about the sex?"

"Later," said Chiun.

"You know, Chiun, sometimes I could kill you."

"Good. We will practice that after supper. And heights, too. You must learn heights. You will learn heights. Heights."

"My mind is on something lower than a belly button, to tell you the truth."

"Then don't tell me the truth," said Chiun. He had made his decision. They would go on as long as they could. Unless of course devious Smith tried something new. He did not tell Remo all the plans Smith had for him. That would be too sad. And besides, who knew if Remo would survive the heights?

In the morning, they went to a seaside part of this gigantic city of the west. Remo needed more training outside the room. It was a place unlike great Roman arenas because people were not killed on purpose here. It was not a park, although it was called that, because there were no trees, or plants like the English or French had in their parks. They called it an amusement park and an island. Coney Island. And like everything else in this land, it was filthy.

Remo and Chiun would take the Ferris wheel. It was the largest Ferris wheel in the world, they said, with the top being more than ten stories above ground.

"This will help you with heights," said Chiun.

"How will riding in a Ferris wheel help me with heights?"

"Who said you were going to ride in it?" said Chiun. "I am going to ride in it."

And Chiun did, as Remo held on to the outside, learning to move between pillars that threatened to crush him as Chiun repeated, "Breathe, very good, that's right, movement breath. Using the air, not wasting it, good. Using the air, using the air."

Remo missed a girder by a hair, crawling up to the side of the cage where Chiun sat with his hands crossed in his lap.

"Jeeesus, Chiun," yelled Remo.

"No prayers. Concentrate," said Chiun, who recognized the name of a western god of the last two thousand years. It helped, when you trained whites, to be familiar with their deities.

Remo crawled up the Ferris wheel cage in which Chiun sat comfortably, to the top, and kept on crawling as the cage made the gigantic circumference.

It was early winter and the amusement park was virtually empty but for the garbage that seemed to infest its lanes and booths. Remo mentioned it might be nice to have a warm coat. Chiun said thank you, but he didn't need one. Remo said it wasn't for Chiun who was inside the cage on the rim of the wheel. Chiun said Remo didn't need one.

Remo said he did. Chiun said he wasn't concentrating. Remo said he didn't care. Chiun said Remo might fall. Remo answered he didn't care about that anymore either.

Good, thought Chiun. He is learning the first thing about heights.

When they were done, Remo in the manner of whites expected a compliment for not getting killed.

"I was pretty good, huh?"

"Because a caterpillar is faster than a flower does not make it a bolt of lightning."

"Am I ever going to do something you think is all right?"

"To be proud of what you do is to look behind you. You must look ahead. You must see what you have to do. An ant can carry one hundred times its own weight. Why?"

"Because you taught him?" said Remo.

"Because he uses his powers fully. You must use your mind. You must believe in your powers. The mind is your power. You must believe."

Remo noticed a stand that openly sold hot dogs, openly sold hamburgers, hamburgers cooked in grease then served with fried onions and tomato catsup alongside, fizzy sugary drinks to wash them down. He was steps away, just upwind from whole hamburgers cooking on a grill.

"I do believe," said Remo. "I believe I am hungry."

"Pale piece of a pig's ear. I cast pearls of wisdom. I attempt transforming, and I get this. But I get what I deserve. You once asked if a Sinanju Master ever had a weakness. I do. My weakness is that I am too nice."

"You already told me that," said Remo, turning away from the hamburgers.

"I will not tolerate these insults anymore."

"You already told me that too."

The two walked to the deserted beach. Remo had to work on his running. The first run sent him dashing across the beach with sand spitting up behind him. He waited at the other end, looking at the watch he had bought despite Chiun's admonition that time was internal not external, that the more one relied on things instead of oneself the more one lost oneself. Look at the appendix. Unused for thirty thousand years, and now useless.

Still there was Remo grinning. Chiun moved to him without haste.

"I swear, I must have done two hundred yards in twelve seconds. That would be a record," said Remo. Chiun looked sadly back at the heavy tracks in the sand.

With great patience he took Remo to where the water covered the smooth sand and then washed back, leaving a flat glistening surface.

"You were not running. You were making holes in the sand. Big banging clumps. Look, there are your footprints. If you wish to kill sand you did well. If you wish to run, run."

"Hey, if you guys are better, then why didn't you enter the Olympics. You could make fortunes running."

"Yes, perhaps this century. Perhaps in the year you called 500 B.C., but those fads change. The world always needs an assassin. Run."

Remo ran down the beach even faster this time. He could see Chiun shake his head.

"No. No. No." Chiun ran to him.

"You were slower than me," said Remo.

"I wanted you to see."

"See what?"

"And you didn't see," said Chiun, pointing to the flat glistening part of the beach where one set of footprints was just being washed by the western sea the whites called the Atlantic.

"You didn't leave footprints," said Remo.

"Ah," said Chiun.

"I am supposed to run without leaving footprints."

"Ah," said Chiun.

"Okay, how do I do it?"

"Now, he asks," said Chiun. "Next time, perhaps, you will help us all by asking beforehand? Yes?"

They practiced running most of the day, until Remo got it almost right. On the way out they passed a ring toss for stuffed dolls, and Chiun won twelve pandas and a Miss Piggy. Remo wanted the Miss Piggy. It reminded him of a long time ago in another life when he had kept it under the dashboard of his squad car. A gang of motorcyclists thought it was funny that two grown men would be carrying dolls. They made comments about the same. Then two of them tried to take away a panda from the elderly oriental.

They were admitted to Brooklyn Mercy Hospital almost as soon as ambulance workers could pry them from the boardwalk of Coney Island. One of them even managed to reach stable condition by midnight.

10

Moscow was burning. The woman shrieked. She wasn't heard. The buzz from below drowned it out. Glasses clinked, people talked. And then Moscow burned itself out and the ash blew away over the crowd gathered beneath the thirty-foot model of the world, where the woman had moments before flicked her cigarette ash so casually. It landed on Moscow because that was near the top of the globe. On the other side, where the partygoers could see from below, was the United States of America, protected by what appeared to be a metallic spider.

The legs, thin glistening wires, were supposed to represent rays. The body was a polished metallic box atop those rays.

"Those rays," explained Mr. Grove's secretary, whose name was Wilson, "will make America and the west invulnerable into the next century."

"We don't want to be invulnerable," said the guest in an accent that sounded vaguely British. He was an official from New Zealand.

"I beg your pardon," said Wilson. Grove Industries had learned long ago that one did not confront pacifists directly, rather one drew them out. At this party in the main ballroom of Grove Industries' Washington office with the elaborate models of the guns, gunships, and now HARP atop the western world, Wilson was performing his duty even if that duty meant making mindless conversation.

George Grove was at this party, and if Wilson could occupy one fool, then that meant one fool less that George Grove had to deal with instead of dealing with congressmen and senators. It was more critical that Grove himself spend time with the people who would be deciding the future of America, which of course meant the future of Grove.

Hearings were under way concerning HARP. Whereas an undiscovered leak would be a problem under any circumstances, Wilson knew so well that a leak now, with HARP coming up, might be disastrous. Exactly why HARP should be more vulnerable than other projects, Wilson honestly did not know.

He was not part of manufacturing. He only did special things for George Grove, like keep this New Zealander occupied.

"Would you explain to me," Wilson asked the man in the good pinstripe suit, somewhat old-fashioned but solidly tailored, "how you could be in danger if we make you invulnerable along with the rest of the west?"

"If the Russians don't think we're invulnerable they won't attack."

"Invulnerable means you can't be harmed."

"That's right, mate. We won't be harmed if we're vulnerable."

"That makes no sense," said Wilson, guiding

the man to the farthest corner of the room where there was a model of one of the first machine guns produced by Grove Industries.

"It don't have to make sense, mate. Do you really think anyone cares what happens to New Zealand; I mean what other civilized country could look up to Australia, mate?"

Wilson had to laugh. The man was right.

"Honest now, right, mate," said the man, refusing a champagne and taking a beer. "No one is going to bother dropping an atomic anything on us. What would they destroy? A bunch of footsoldiers in funny hats? Sheep? Dogs? Horses? A garden party?"

Wilson glanced back at Grove. A general with a beautiful major was approaching Grove, who had a senator cornered. Wilson knew the senator would be crucial to HARP. He knew Grove did not want to be bothered by the military when he was working Congress. The general was approaching at flank speed. But Wilson could not get away from the friendly New Zealander who, as was the manner of his countrymen, talked with an armlock on his listener.

"Look, mate, we know we are not really targets. Could you name me one atomic scientist from Australia? Could you name me one great electronics engineer from New Zealand? Name me something we export that could affect the modern world in any way. Ever see a New Zealand camera or an Australian television set? Getting the picture, mate?"

Wilson tried to break free, but the New Zealander was on a roll. "Name me anything that ever came out of New Zealand but our national beer. And there ain't no place, mate, what don't have its national beer. And what's neighbor Australia known for? What is the one thing that continent down under has done? Name it. You know it."

Wilson watched the general and the major close in. Mr. Grove had wanted congressional time at this party. In fact, that was the party's purpose. He could see that General Scott Watson anytime. And certainly there was no major in the world that would do anything but take up Mr. Grove's valuable congressional time. But the New Zealander held Wilson fast.

"Name it, mate. All right, I'll tell you. We won a bloody boat race, that's what. A sailboat race. Australia's great technological breakthrough was a bloody keel. They've been coming up with new keels since the Stone Age. Do you know how you tell an aborigine from the prime ministers of New Zealand and Australia?"

Wilson tried a smile and a duck and a good-bye but the New Zealander was too swift for him.

"The difference between the Stone Age aborigine and our elected leaders, mate, can be most readily discerned by turning on the lights. Aborigines are black."

The New Zealander gave himself a hearty laugh. Wilson was now faced with the horrible dilemma of risking a seam tear in his jacket or watching George Grove lose vital lobbying time. Wilson ripped. The New Zealander let go. Wilson's unrestrained arm went sailing into someone's back, knocking a drink into someone else's face.

"Ever taste our New Zealand lamb?"

"No, dammit," yelled Wilson, who saw now he had failed. The general and the major had arrived at George Grove. He knew this because George Grove was faking a friendly smile.

"Mr. Grove, this is our Major Rayner Fleming

of whom we are most proud," said General Watson. "Major Fleming, George Grove."

General Watson waited for George Grove's charm to work. The message was clear. George Grove for some reason was to turn this young lady's head.

"My, my," said George Grove. "If all the majors look like you, I'm joining the Army again."

General Watson thought that was tremendously funny. He laughed. Grove laughed. Major Fleming maintained a polite silence.

"Major Fleming is our best in-house watchdog," said General Watson. "She keeps the world honest. And we're grateful for it."

"Really, Major Fleming," said Grove, impressed. "What do you watch?"

"Oh, you know. The usual defense-contract stuff. Fraud. Waste. Shoddy workmanship. The AR-60," said Major Fleming.

"AR what?"

"The field rifle Grove manufactures," said General Watson.

"Oh, that. Yes, well, forgive me. My mind is on HARP," said Grove, nodding to the world whose western half was protected by the metallic simulations of electronic rays. "We can make every city, every home in America safe with that."

"If you can't make a rifle correctly how can you make an electronics space defense?" said Major Fleming.

General Watson started to answer, but Grove was going to handle this one himself.

"We are really so vast that different factories, different staffs produce different equipment. One has nothing to do with the other."

"I would say that they do. Quality control is quality control. We lost a man with one of your lousy rifles. Now I hear that thing is being billed as America's roof," said Major Fleming, nodding to the metallic box with the metallic spider-leg rays suspended over the room. "Well, how do we know it is not going to leak?"

George Grove was going to answer that one when unfortunately an assistant of his named Wilson insisted he immediately had to go over to speak to an Undersecretary of Defense.

"I'm sorry, I have to go," said Grove. He nodded his good intentions with a warm smile, as though if given time, none of them really would see a problem at all, especially the major who was upset.

"His name was Anthony D'Amico, Mr. Grove," said Major Fleming.

"Excuse me?" said George Grove, following his elbow which was being tugged away by his aide, Wilson.

"The soldier who died testing your junk rifle. Private Anthony D'Amico," yelled Major Fleming.

"I'm sorry," said Grove, and when he was out of hearing distance, whispered, "What took you so long?"

"I was trapped by a New Zealander telling me everything that was wrong with New Zealand and Australia."

"You're lucky you got out this century. Who is that Major Rayner Fleming?"

"I don't know. I am sure she must be someone on General Watson's staff."

"She mentioned the AR-60."

"The leak?"

"If it's not us, it must be them."

"General Watson is careful about that. He may not know a bullet from a brassiere, but the man is an American flag officer. He does understand the danger of the press, even if he doesn't always move quickly enough for you."

"I know people, Wilson. That woman is upset. And she would leak. Warn Scott Watson about her. I don't know what's the matter with him for not spotting her himself. I would bet she was the officer who pushed through that bad AR-60 report also."

Wilson nodded. Normally Grove himself would be the conduit to General Watson. But George Grove did not want to spare the time now. The future phases of HARP were coming up before Congress now, and the head of Grove Industries could not be bothered with a simple little rifle, or some major who was obsessed with it. Besides, if worse came to worst, Grove Industries could always manufacture the AR-60 properly no matter how much that would cut into profits.

At the other end of the room, General Watson was furious.

"Major, I am afraid that display at a Washington party will do little to advance your career," said General Watson.

"My father fought all across Europe. He served in Korea. He fought in Vietnam. Three wars, and every time he went into battle he knew he had the best equipment his government could give him. We didn't do the same for Private D'Amico. I went to his funeral. I made a promise to his grandfather, who fought for another country a long time ago. They did not go into battle with the best weapons."

"I see," said General Watson. When Grove's man Wilson saw Watson the next day, the general told him:

"None of us will have to worry about Major Fleming anymore. I will not even have to mention that she spoke without permission to the press."

"I would like to know what you are going to do. We want discretion about all things. We are not that concerned with the AR-60 in itself. That is not the major weapons system."

"Don't worry. I know a psychological case when I see one," said General Watson. "She has difficulty working with people and unfortunately, she became too emotionally involved after seeing a soldier's death. Now we all care about our brave men, but this officer went to the man's funeral, even though he was not in her outfit. And I was there at a Washington party when she wildly called out his name to a manufacturer who wasn't even all that familiar with that small product. She needs a rest, Wilson."

"Very good," said Wilson. He noticed the array of campaign ribbons on General Watson's uniform. The uniform, Wilson had to admit to himself, didn't do much for the man. The last really good uniform was that of the British Hussars, 1702 to 1755, but he doubted whether the American military would be interested in tassels nowadays.

Major Rayner Fleming knew her career might be over, and not because of calling a name out at a party. She knew it might be over because, faced with removal from monitoring the quality of the AR-60 and being ordered to a military clinic for "stress examination," she defied orders.

She did not report to the hospital.

She took a very big risk, one she calculated had one chance in twenty. Alone, she went to an Undersecretary of Defense and took on one of the largest defense contractors.

"I believe, sir," she said, "that Grove Industries is unqualified to manufacture arms for the United States military. I believe that in a barrel of generally good apples, providing the best military equipment in the world, this manufacturer provides rot. And I suspect that it is rotten throughout, and that it lives on rotting whatever it touches."

The meeting was held in a small office with a view of the Potomac. A picture of an aircraft carrier hung behind the Undersecretary. Private D'Amico's rifle looked like a very small thing in this office, where models of missiles sat on the desk, where problems affecting hundreds of thousands of men were solved.

But that rifle and that private were Major Fleming's business. Even if this man might not remember the name of anyone with less than two stars, this lowly major had to do what she had to do.

The problem was apparent immediately. General Watson had outsmarted her.

"You say that you have been sent to a clinic for rest. I am sure your file will verify that. You say your problem is stress?"

"Yes," said Major Fleming. She noticed the Undersecretary's eyes glance lightly at her breasts and then move on up to her face. "My problem is listed as stress, but the real problem is that I give a damn."

"That's a serious charge, Major."

"I understand that."

"And you have bucked this out of channels, around your commanding officer?"

"Correct."

"This could get you court-martialed, you know. There are channels. You could make a report."

"And have it destroyed by the master of reports. General Watson is the best bureaucratic infighter in Washington. He may not remember who won World War Two or why, or what to do when an enemy is about to turn your flank on a battlefield, but he damned well knows how to wield a mean memo."

"That is a further serious charge against your commanding officer. I would call it defamation."

"And I would call it accurate."

"Nothing you have done today here in my office with these unsubstantiated charges would indicate that General Watson was not absolutely right. It appears from your extremely tense demeanor and wild charges that you do indeed suffer from stress. Now, I will attribute all of this to your malady and let you go on to your rest. I know how hard and tension-filled a job like yours can be."

Major Fleming inhaled deeply. The Undersecretary was letting her walk back off the limb. She could say forget everything, go to a hospital for a few weeks, come out with a clean bill of health and resume her career. Or she could do otherwise.

"No," she said. "I stand by it all."

The Undersecretary nodded, somewhat sadly. This beautiful officer had just all but scuttled her career. He almost wished she was right about Grove Industries and General Watson. Because what she had done just now was say to the United States government, it was either her or them.

"I will accept a written statement from you on this matter," said the Undersecretary, "and then I would advise you to proceed to that hospital."

He paused and then with a sigh said:

"I'm sorry. That is all I can do."

It was them.

* * *

Ordinarily Major Fleming's report would not go far beyond her own file to provide proof that her commanding officer had made the right decision in dismissing her. It would get a review from a board, and the board would find her "hysterical," a term more loosely used for women than men.

But on this particular board was someone who had orders to forward all reports, no matter how unsubstantiated, to a file in one of the many monitor offices in Washington.

He was not sure exactly what it was. Someone told him once, but that didn't matter. The important thing was filing this report in a computer-coded manner, one of many computer-coded manners he filed reports in all day long. He didn't know where the others went for certain, and therefore felt little concern for this report's destination either.

The Fleming report, however, had what were called "flags." A program seeing one of these flags would pick up the report and forward it. The Fleming report had three strong flags.

One, it concerned the AR-60, for which a flag had been set.

Two, it concerned Grove Industries, for which another flag had been set.

And three, it set a flag for anyone reporting malfeasance concerning the above two items.

Within a microsecond the screen of Harold W. Smith, in that Wall Street cover, was alight with an interruption. He had personally set the flags. As he read the report on Major Fleming, his native New England reserve contained his excitement.

What Harold W. Smith had discovered was

what he had seen in so many branches of the armed forces despite general opinion to the contrary. An officer was ready to go all the way for what she believed. But what excited Harold W. Smith was that now he had the one person to use against Grove, inside the system. If the major were willing to risk her career without good informational support, then she certainly was not going to break under any other pressure and she certainly was not going to be bought off.

Good for you, Major Fleming, thought Smith. You're the one real man in that command.

If Smith were a whistler, he would have whistled that day as he worked. He created orders and counterorders. He created a whole system that had not only cleared Major Fleming of any sign of emotional weakness, but added a merit report, and transferred her neatly away from General Scott Watson, whose name would now be flagged on anything to do with malfeasance.

And even better yet, Major Fleming would not be alone anymore. She would get all the support she needed even though she would never know where it came from.

The orders arrived at the hospital before Major Fleming. She was not to be treated at the hospital, but return to Washington to join the staff of the Joint Chiefs. And she was ordered to investigate two projects. The AR-60, and one to do with the Air Force, perhaps the most glamorous defense project in the history of the nation, HARP, America's roof against the nuclear rain.

George Grove, because he ate sparingly, rarely felt like vomiting. But this day in the crucial congressional subcommittee hearing in Washington, he wanted to vomit up the salad and mineral water he had eaten for breakfast. Then he wanted to strangle Wilson. And maybe General Scott Watson, as well.

Walking to the opposite side of the table set before the congressional bench in the closed-door meeting was the major Wilson had promised Watson would get rid of. She arrived with a thick sheaf of notes. Grove forced himself not to look at her, to pay attention to the Air Force officer's smooth presentation on why America should move forward from HARP I system into HARP II.

It was winter and the good Jamaica tan hid Grove's seething red rage.

"And so," concluded the Air Force officer's excellent presentation, "I can only reiterate, Mr. Chairman, that the HARP system is a key element in our defensive shield in space . . ."

Grove nodded sagely. The chairman, a representative from Chillicothe, Ohio, glanced at his watch. He had heard this presentation many times before. He figured the officer could wind up now in time for everyone to take two good stiff cocktails before dinner.

"I think everyone in this room," said the officer, "shares a dream. A dream that one day our nation will be invulnerable to nuclear attack."

The chairman whispered to the representative on his left about the quality of the winter heating in the Capitol. He noticed the contractor was nodding. He was supposed to. He noticed the other Air Force officers were paying rapt attention, even though they probably had brainstormed every comma in the report. But one strange thing was happening at the testimony table. An Army officer was taking notes, quite seriously.

And other members of the committee were watching her.

"What a pair, huh?" whispered another representative.

"Her and who?" asked the chairman, also in a whisper.

"Them on her," answered the other representative.

"I don't like the heating in here," whispered the chairman, who knew the presentation almost as well as the Air Force officer. This whole thing was a foregone conclusion. America was as committed to HARP as it was to electing its national leaders.

"HARP," said the Air Force officer, his pointer resting on a chart of America's space borders, "can bring us closer to that dream in our search for the ultimate weapon of peace. I recommend that we proceed to system level development on HARP II with all possible speed. Thank you."

Good, thought the chairman. We are all going to make cocktails tonight. It was over. The other congressmen were gathering their papers when he said:

"I think we're all agreed then. If there are no objections—"

"Mr. Chairman. There is one point I'd like to raise," said the beautiful major.

Grove tasted the watercress come up, and swallowed it back down with his anger.

"We are all aware of the strategic importance of the HARP system to our national defense. But I question the advisability of pouring money into HARP II when we haven't seen anything of HARP I yet."

There was silence in the closed hearing. Two congressmen on their way to the door sat back down at their table. Everyone looked to Grove and the Air Force officers.

"If I may be permitted to ask Mr. Grove a question," Major Fleming asked.

"Yes, yes. Go ahead," said the chairman. He was down to a single cocktail that night, he knew.

"Mr. Grove, can you tell us what the delay is in making HARP I operational?"

Grove exuded competence and just a little bit of annoyance in his answer.

"Of course, I can tell you," he said, looking at the congressmen and not at the major. "It's committees like this that take a sound design, chew it up and spit it back with a lot of new specs attached."

George Grove looked directly at one of his good friends when he said this, and his good friend did not let him down.

"George has a point," said the congressman, now bouncing the ball into the Air Force court. "You generals can't blink without coming up with a hundred new design demands."

"Which naturally adds to cost overruns. But my question is even more troubling. It is vital and basic. When can we see anything of the HARP I we have paid so much for?"

George Grove slammed down a file.

"Mr. Chairman," he said with properly controlled rage. "My company has one of the finest track records in this town . . . What about the CD-18, Major? Three months ahead of schedule. And under budget. We don't hear about under-budgets, do we? We don't hear of bettering a deadline, either. That CD-18 will be ready for testing next week. Next week. Not next month. Next week."

"Yes, at Mount Promise, I am aware of that. That is one of General Watson's programs. I will be there too. If you do know him personally, as I suspect, please do tell him I will be there."

Trapped, George Grove fell back on his patriotism. He questioned Major Fleming's questioning it. He questioned Congress's questioning it. He questioned anyone questioning it. Finally, the chairman had to say no one was questioning it.

"I think the question was about HARP I. And it was a good one," said the chairman of the congressional subcommittee.

"Damn good," said another congressman. He was not one of George Grove's friends.

Outside the hearing room, Wilson was waiting.

"How did it go?"

"Do you remember the major at the party?"

"Yes. Watson got rid of her."

"Yes, out of his stinking little command right to the Joint Chiefs and HARP."

"Oh, no," said Wilson.

"She is out. Out. Out. Out."

"I understand."

"I am not talking about a head cold or a transfer."

"I understand."

"Use the best. I don't want to see that face again on this earth."

"Not a problem, George," said Wilson.

"I knew she would be trouble."

"No problem," said Wilson.

"She was supposed to be no problem before. And now I see her looking across from me at what was supposed to be an open-and-shut hearing, that now has stayed open."

"No problem. I smell the handiwork of our enemies behind the wall I noticed. If you know me, you know I am going to get them," said Wilson. "So what is the problem?"

Grove thought a moment, letting the steam subside.

"I am going to use Stone on her," said Wilson.

"Okay. Good then. All right," said George Grove. He ignored the major as she walked out of the hearing room deep in conversation with one of the congressmen. He would rather see her talking to that one than someone who wasn't bought.

11

Harold W. Smith could not get the answer from even his organization's computers. No numbers, nor any logic system could answer his question that day. The answer was not there and never had been. He left the office, quite safely since only he had the codes to access anything in it, and went for a walk on the streets of New York shortly before lunch. He went to the Battery and looked out over the waters wondering, on this cold winter day, whether it would all work or not.

They were so few. The enemy was so many. What could he tell the President? He had already been given a killer arm.

"Give me another, sir, this one won't be ready for a decade and if we use him we will lose him."

The purpose of having one was to use him. McCleary was limited. True, underneath the casual beer-drinking wisecracker was a patriot who had taken the same vow Smith had taken, one never before asked of any American servicemen or agents. It was an oath Remo did not know about yet, and with luck Smith would never have to tell him.

Smith looked out at the Statue of Liberty under repair. The salt water did not clear his head or make his decision any easier. Was it because of the garbage washing up against the city shore, or was it the fact that he really didn't have an answer yet about Remo?

McCleary had already seen the young man dodge a bullet. He already could trail McCleary, an experienced agent, without McCleary knowing he was behind him.

So why was Smith so troubled about using Remo?

He breathed deeply, and smelled the coffee grounds and rotting orange skins. He turned away from America's major eastern harbor. The answer was not out in the water. It was in him.

He and McCleary had volunteered. He and McCleary had taken the terrible vow because of their love of country.

Remo had been given a psychological test and then kidnapped.

Harold W. Smith did not trust Remo. It was that simple.

He walked back to his office on nearby Wall Street. He had faced what was bothering him, and the rest was easy. He had been delaying Remo's use because he felt Remo, when put to the ultimate challenge of laying his life on the line, might not come through.

Harold W. Smith, the very dry man of numbers, did not trust psychological tests. He trusted men. He trusted McCleary. He trusted himself. Remo so far was just a probability, a probability who was going to have to be trusted sometime. If he should fly the coop, back off, or fail in some other way, better that it happened now than two years from now. Better have Chiun finish the contract and go home to North Korea where no one in America would hear from him again.

The way he told it to McCleary later that day was:

"Well, let's see what we have."

McCleary would never know the struggle that had gone on within Smith before he was able to say those words.

"I was wondering what was holding you up," said McCleary. "I would like to see that myself—see what he does when the feces hit the air conditioning. I feel like he's mine, you know. I named him. Mine."

"That's what we are going to find out tomorrow," said Smith. "Just who our Remo does belong to."

Chiun had brought Remo back to the Coney Island beach. The running was correct now. Westerners might call it perfect, but that perfection was a strange western concept. It was a way of judging.

Chiun was not here to judge. He was here to give Remo correctness. Perhaps that was the key to those lingering problems in Remo. He thought in wrong ways. How Chiun wished at that moment that he could have gotten to Remo before the rest of his race did. Then Remo might not be turning around after each exercise to ask how he did.

It was such a strange thing, thought Chiun.

Remo would do something and then ask how he did. When told there was one thing or another that was wrong, he would answer:

"Yeah, but it's still pretty good. I don't know of anyone else but you or me who could do that."

And that response was a puzzlement. He wanted approval for performing incorrectly. Granted, there were many things he did just as instructed. But when you started complimenting, where would it end?

Such as not allowing the gun to be successful against you. Remo was happy now that he could dodge three bullets in a row. But he should have six at least, which he did not.

The delay in his progress began as soon as Remo had succeeded with two or three bullets. His mind started judging then, saying he was good. He needed not to think. He needed not to judge. What a bad influence that McCleary had been, telling him how amazed he was at Remo's feat.

McCleary could well get him killed with talk like that.

Chiun watched Remo move across the slick wet sand.

Correct. Not the slightest indentation of a toeprint.

"All right, do it with the water," said Chiun, and Remo was laughing.

"You want me to walk on water? I knew you would ask that someday," said Remo.

He was laughing. The laughter was infectious. His growing skill was infectious. The light of the star Chiun had seen months before, when first he examined the first clumsy movements, shone brightly now.

Yet, Chiun was Master of Sinanju, and his first loyalty was to the village of Sinanju. He could not let himself feel too deeply for this one. The devious Emperor Smith had provided the gold. Remo belonged to Smith, not to Chiun. On the other hand, what had Smith taught Remo?

Remo was still laughing at his own jest, referring to a miracle performed by a god in a western religion. Knowing whites so well, Chiun could appreciate these little asides.

"Sand," said Chiun, and nodded to the next exercise.

"I don't know if I am ready," said Remo.

"Then you are not ready."

"Well, why don't you say that about heights when I think I am not ready?"

"Because your fear of heights you had naturally as a child. It will always be there. It has to be overcome. The exercise through the sand is something else. It is next in a natural progression of skills."

"I think I'm ready," said Remo.

He wore shorts and a light T-shirt and no shoes. His breath made clouds in the air. Chiun wore a light gray morning kimono. Remo understood now how Chiun could not be cold on a cold winter day. The human body could warm itself. It was just that most people had to run around to raise their temperature to counteract the loss of heat through the skin on cold days. But when one became one with himself, and gained control of the mind and the will through breathing, one merely raised one's temperature as needed. That was Sinanju and it seemed so easy that Remo wondered how there could have been a time he could not do this.

The white sand was cold under his feet but not a penetrating cold. Sea gulls cawed and perched on nearby wharves. The sky was winter gray, and no one strolled the boardwalk. Remo tasted his own breath which was clean and pure. Better than that. It was correct. He was correct.

He knew the sand and he knew himself, and his body moved on the first toe of the first foot, leaving the sand slightly. Then, above the sand, he moved, quite cleanly, seeing a place ahead where the grains of sand formed a goodly mass, and then down, down with more force than any kick would allow, head first into the grains of sand, cutting deep into the place where the sand was dark and still warm from yesterday's sun. Then, with one jackknife of his midsection, Remo turned upward toward the air, up out of the sand, bursting free like a dolphin through the water and running.

If there had been an observer on the boardwalk he would have blinked several times and wondered whether to tell anyone what he saw. A man had moved along the sand faster than any sprinter, and then as though it were water, dove into the sand, and come up out of it without missing a beat.

Chiun saw Remo stop and turn around.

"Too much leg," said Chiun.

Remo stuck his tongue between his lips and made a derogatory noise.

"You help. You give, and this is what you get for it. Thank you, Remo."

"I thought I did pretty well," said Remo.

"What is pretty well? What is this white talk? Pretty well? Are you fairly alive? Is someone mostly dead? What is this?"

"Well I thought it was good. I did well."

"I am insulted for helping," said Chiun, "and then the help is refused. Why ask me? What do you want from me?"

"I'd like approval," said Remo.

"All right. Your legs did not do too much of the work. It was correct."

"No. I don't mean that," said Remo. "I'd like to hear a nice word now and then."

"Nice word," said Chiun, chuckling, even though Remo didn't seem to appreciate a good joke.

"You know, people improve when they get encouragement," said Remo.

"I thought you said you were doing pretty well. Why, that is better than almost well, and it is close to fairly wonderful," said Chiun. Chiun had made another joke. Remo was unable to appreciate that, too.

They returned home for dinner, and Remo was waiting for the rice, though not because he wanted to eat it. Eating had lost its pleasure. He only hoped the same thing would not happen to his sex drive. But when the rice was put before him, he took one mouthful and spit it out.

"Awful. You make lousy rice. You are the worst cook I ever tasted. I know oriental dishes and you are totally inferior, Master of Sinanju."

"Why do you say that?" said Chiun.

"Because it is not correct," said Remo. "Don't expect compliments for almosts and partiallys. You served not correct rice."

"Why do you say that?" asked Chiun again.

"Because it tastes like cement and cow dung," said Remo.

"Then your taste is wrong," said Chiun. "Another failing of yours that I must work on." Remo walked away from his rice.

"You really know how to be insulting, don't you," said Chiun. He proceeded to eat his rice in dignified silence. Remo asked if Chiun were truly insulted. Chiun allowed as how he most certainly was, when Remo walked away from his rice.

Chiun did not understand why this made Remo happy, happy enough to eat his rice, but then all whites were strange.

"Sometimes, people who do not appreciate good rice like it cooked with vinegar. The Japanese eat it with vinegar," said Chiun.

That evening Con McCleary came to the training house and told Remo the first assignment would be the next day. He asked Chiun what he thought.

"Taste this rice," said Chiun.

"I've eaten, Master of Sinanju. I just came for Remo. We are going to use him tomorrow. Nothing I think too dangerous."

"Try the rice," said Chiun.

The lacquered bowl was before McCleary's face and he couldn't refuse.

"Okay," he said, and with the chopsticks Chiun provided pressed a small ball of white sticky rice together and ate it.

"What do you think?" asked Chiun.

"It's rice," said McCleary. Remo leaned against a wall grinning with his arms folded.

"Good rice. Fairly good rice. Correct rice?"

"Yeah. Rice. Correct."

"Of course," said Chiun. "But some fools don't know that. See, Remo. Even this alcohol-drugged meat-eating wretch knows correct rice when he eats it."

And Chiun motioned to Remo while talking to McCleary. "This thing without taste buds you give me to train. There is nothing he knew. Not breathing, and not even how to taste."

"I didn't like his cooking," said Remo.

"There is nothing imperfect with my cooking," said Chiun.

"We've got work tomorrow," said McCleary.

"I have made rice longer than either of you have lived."

"There is some danger but I think we can avoid it," said McCleary. "We are basically going to protect a woman in the Army, a woman who is doing her job."

"Rice is supposed to stick together and have taste, not be some tasteless form of separate-grain mush this one is used to," said Chiun.

"We'd like your thinking on this, Master of Sinanju," said McCleary. Remo's grin was growing wider.

The situation was this. The organization had discovered that a Major Rayner Fleming might be the target of a hit when she went to the auditor general's office the next day. What McCleary and Remo would do would be to make sure she lived through the next day. And longer.

"Who is going to try to do the hit, do you know?"

"A very powerful organization, one the taxpayers support, Grove Industries. She is a threat to them."

"How do you know they are going to do a hit?"

"We don't for sure," said McCleary. "We pick up things. Smitty has got to be a damned computer genius. What the computers do is flag things, things that might not seem odd piece by piece but when put together, have to be looked into. We know Major Fleming is a danger to Grove's profits. We don't yet know how dangerous her enemies are, but we suspect they would kill. They do spread money around rather shrewdly."

"But the hit?" asked Remo. "How do you know about that?"

"All right. Grove's private lines are accessed. Bugs if you want. There is this super errand boy of George Grove's named Wilson. No other name. Makes a fortune for salary. We pick up a phone call from him, and his voice just mentions a time. Millions of calls are picked up, but the computer flags this one. And there are just three words in the whole conversation. An airline, a flight number, and a day. Nothing much, right?"

Remo nodded. Chiun looked at McCleary's chopsticks.

"But the call is to a man named Stone. Now I don't know if you are aware how vast this computer system is, but in the billions of bytes, there is a flag set for this man named Stone, who we believed was working in North Africa. He is always a flag. He is a killer, a bit of a sadist to boot. But you take the phone call to Stone from Wilson of Grove and you add it to the flight schedule of our Major Rayner Fleming who is taking that precise flight on that precise day to go to the auditor general's office in New York City, and you get a probable hit by Grove Industries using Stone to kill Fleming."

"And what if it's not? What if this guy Wilson intends to take the flight himself tomorrow and wants to be met at the airport?"

"Then our good friend Major Fleming is not in danger. We want her alive."

"I see," said Remo. He looked at his hands. He had never killed with them before. Supposedly when he reached the full use of his powers he would never need a weapon again. He was the weapon.

"Are you ready?" asked McCleary.

"Sure," said Remo, with a grin. "Ready or not, here we come, breathing all the way."

"And you, Chiun? What do you think?" asked McCleary.

"You didn't finish your rice," said Chiun.

"I've had dinner," said McCleary.

"It needed vinegar," said Chiun.

"No. It was good. It was good."

"Take one chopstick full," said Chiun.

"One," said McCleary. And he downed a ball of rice and gave Chiun a big smile, assuring him this was just about the best rice he had ever eaten.

"Then why are you leaving it?" asked the Master of Sinanju.

Reginald Stone did not believe in tailing someone like a lost puppy, afraid of losing a scent. For one thing, a traffic light, a minor auto accident, any number of things could snap a tail. And if you attempted to keep it despite interruptions, you attracted attention.

Reginald Stone did not like to attract attention. It was unnecessary. And unprofessional. If one knew where a target was going to be, it was easier to wait, and let the target come to you.

And so he waited in a car outside the auditor general's office in New York City, careful to check that no one lay in wait for him, although that was highly unlikely.

He ran his tongue over his diamond tooth. Somehow that diamond always reassured him in moments like these, reminding him of his power and skill.

A hot-dog vendor collected money with one hand as he shoveled sauerkraut atop a frankfurter on a roll with the other. Stone watched the movements. Too skilled for an undercover cop. Too concerned about the change.

A single policeman struggled to direct traffic down the street. A traffic cop. No problem there.

Stone's blond good looks got him a few stares from women. He didn't let them make eye contact. He might not be able to get rid of them.

A stunning woman in army green walked smartly up the street. Reginald Stone touched his diamond tooth again with his tongue, and leaned his buttonhole slightly out the window. He squeezed a rubber ball inside his coat pocket. He heard a click under his lapel. He squeezed again. He heard another click.

He had just taken two pictures of Major Rayner Fleming entering the auditor general's office. Then he sat back and waited. He liked working with Wilson. Unlike most people who taught themselves most of their trade, he was thorough. Wilson did not panic. He wanted pictures. He wanted to make sure of everyone around the point of attack.

Wilson was a compulsive about information. Stone had suggested a simple little kill. Wilson had refused. So Stone gave him his photos. If that's what Wilson wanted, Stone would not argue. He'd had worse employers.

Libya for one. The money was good. It was afterward, talking to their state committee for security, that showed what true amateurs they were. The Libyans felt they had not only a right to kill their enemies but also a duty to brag about it. They wanted details. They wanted pictures of the victims in pain. How different it was for Wilson. He wanted pictures only to make absolutely sure who was who where and when.

Wilson's genius was pure simplicity. Where could one conduct a torture operation with absolutely no one questioning the administration of pain? A hospital. Wilson had one near every major Grove plant. All Stone had to do was show up in a white coat. Then he could "treat" a patient in whatever manner he felt most effective.

Wilson was that good.

Stone felt the hardness of the diamond in his mouth. He had taken it that wonderful day when he realized what he should do with the rest of his life.

It was in North Africa. A revolutionary group had discovered the best possible way to establish good press relations. What you did was kill anyone who wrote bad things about you. Just let your annoyance be known, then kill them. There might be an article or two about it, but nothing really big in the Middle East. Reporters would become quite wary before writing anything negative. On the other hand, the countries that got into trouble with the press were those that treated them openly, such as in a democracy. They got lambasted all the time, especially since it became fashionable to do so, and totally free of danger.

This policy worked magnificently for the most ruthless of dictatorships, and of course some of it was Stone's work. He was obviously not Arab, and therefore correspondents would let down their guard. His first kill was an American reporter for a midwest newspaper. She was worried because she had written extensively about the massacre at Hama, a Syrian town which was annihilated for opposing the government. Estimates had it that twenty thousand people were killed, or roughly sixty times more than were killed in Sabra and Shatilla camps by Lebanese Maronites.

The difference between the two was that Sabra and Shatilla were in Israeli-occupied territory and Hama was not. There could be a news angle indirectly blaming Israel. That was safe. And fashionable, although as massacres went it wasn't even in the top ten of the year in the Middle East.

But this young reporter believed in facts, and stubbornly insisted upon writing about Hama.

Stone befriended her, even told her of a safe place in the mountains where they could lunch. Nothing sexual. Just two friends. Besides, she was engaged anyhow.

He took her into the mountains one fine morning and shot her eyes out of her head. It was beautiful.

To remind himself of his success, he took her engagement ring and had the diamond mounted in his tooth. Ever since then, when working, Stone always got comfort from running his tongue over its facets. He had done it eighty-seven times. He had eighty-seven hits. There was no reason why, on this day in New York City, he would not make it eighty-eight.

Suddenly he looked around. Was someone watching him?

Con McCleary knew how to wear an officer's uniform. He had served three years as an airborne officer in Vietnam before joining the CIA. The colonel's uniform felt just like his captain's uniform. Awful.

Con McCleary hated uniforms. He had a theory about them. People wore uniforms so they could disguise themselves as soldiers.

"Major Fleming is here, Colonel," said the secretary.

"Send her in," said McCleary, reminding himself not to appear as though he enjoyed what he was doing. He never remembered a colonel enjoying what he did. Sergeants enjoyed what they did, and generals seemed to enjoy at least a speech or two, or a command decision under pressure, but Con McCleary never remembered a colonel who had fun.

This was hard to affect the moment he saw Major Rayner Fleming. Her full body and stunning smooth skin made him wonder if, as a colonel, he could order this major to take off her clothes. Maybe threaten court-martial if she failed to make love as ordered.

He dismissed these lovely thoughts from his mind with a simple salute. His job now was to keep her in his office until Remo got into position. Stone had been spotted outside in the street.

Major Fleming saluted. McCleary returned the salute.

"I believe we have the documents you requested," he said.

"I didn't know that a colonel was in charge of them. I thought a captain would sign them over."

"Well, sometimes captains have difficulty getting access to things."

"Captains aren't the only ones. HARP seems to be the most difficult access file I have ever seen. Those who are supposed to have authorization need someone else to confirm, and so on. Even the normal financial reports are somehow always hiding in another computer. I don't even know how you got the reports."

"Make sure they're right," said McCleary, handing her a sheaf of computer printouts.

"Here? Now?"

"Yes, and of course sign for them."

Major Fleming looked at her watch. Con McCleary looked at Major Fleming looking at her watch, or thereabouts. He wondered if he were to unbutton her blouse with his tongue if he would go on report. Since he was using cover rank and cover name, no report could harm him.

"Yes. This is it. This is what we need. How did you get it? How do you have access codes that the Joint Chiefs don't have?"

"Military secret," said McCleary. He wondered if he should tell her she was the most wonderful woman he ever met, his one true contact in the great void of all eternity. He only had ten minutes at most, though. Remo would have scouted the area and been in position by then. Con McCleary needed at least a good half an evening to establish his deepest relationships.

Ironically, he had a personality trait similar to that which distinguished Remo's profile—an inability to form a lasting relationship with a member of the opposite sex—but for the converse reasons. Remo couldn't sustain a long relationship because he cared too much, almost drove women away in his previous life. McCleary didn't care about the next day. On the sea of love, Remo plunged to the depths too quickly, and McCleary floated into the clouds, neither of them ever moving smoothly across the surface for any length of time.

"Yes. This is what I need. But these are the strangest figures I have ever seen for a project. Do you understand the implications?" asked Major Fleming.

McCleary glanced at the numbers. Not a decimal, he thought. "We assumed they would prove useful," he said. He went to the window. Remo had just entered the building. "You can read them all back in Washington," he said.

"How did you access these records?"

"I am not at liberty to say. Good day, Major,"

said McCleary, wondering briefly if he might give her a more personal good-bye.

It was, of course, Smith who had broken into parts of the HARP file using the information McCleary had sneaked out of Grove in Washington after his stint as an Internal Revenue Service examiner. There would be more information forthcoming, to be relayed directly to Major Fleming's terminal in Washington.

If Major Fleming had met the real colonel in charge of this section of the auditor general's office, as she had planned, she would have gotten one solid stone wall, not because he wasn't doing his job, but because he was doing his job legally.

She also might have gotten killed. She still might, thought McCleary.

He would wait two minutes so that he would be sure of not coming in contact with Remo. If Remo got into trouble he would not help. He had to get out of this uniform and building as quickly as possible. That was the secret of not getting caught. You moved quickly in and out. Funny, he thought. That was also the secret of his love life.

Major Fleming could have sworn the elevator doors were shut when they banged open again. She instinctively protected her briefcase.

The man shot her a smile. He had high cheekbones, was somewhat thin, with a craggy sort of face. Dark eyes. He was smiling at her as though he knew her.

"Hi," he said.

"Hello," she said, and immediately broke eye contact.

"That's a nice uniform," said Remo.

"Yes, a whole army wears them," said Major

Fleming. Why did she always seem to get these types on elevators?

"Are you putting me down?" asked Remo. This was his variation of a sexual technique Chiun had mentioned briefly only to illustrate the proper footwork necessary when approaching a wall. Chiun called it accosting. Of course, correctly done, accosting had to do with the Korean festival of the blossom and you were supposed to be dancing at the time. It was harder to pull off in an elevator.

The major did not answer him.

"Nice buttons on the uniform," said Remo. He had never been good at elevator conversations, and establishing contact under orders was even more cumbersome. And what made it worse, she seemed like a nice decent woman, the sort of woman he would have liked to meet if this weren't work. What a stupid remark about the buttons, he thought.

She didn't answer that either.

"I like elevators," said Remo. Did he actually say that? It was even more stupid than the previous comment.

Major Fleming looked at her watch, as though timing the descent.

"No, really I find them very . . . stimulating," said Remo. His mouth said that, though no human brain, he thought, could have come up with it.

She still didn't answer, and since he couldn't back off now, he continued.

"Something about the small enclosed space . . . the smooth walls . . . the tight air . . . the canned music . . ."

Major Fleming smiled. It was too much. She couldn't help herself.

"Okay, not the music," said Remo.

"Enjoy your ups and downs," said Major Fleming as the doors opened. Remo followed her out of the elevator, out of the building onto the street. She was trying to get away from him, walking very quickly across the street to a car that seemed to be ready to offer her a lift. But something was strange about the driver. She couldn't tell just what it was until she realized his mouth glinted in the sun. He had a large diamond set in a front tooth.

12

Remo moved right into the street, getting a hand on Major Fleming's briefcase and holding her with it, securely but not with a jerk that would have knocked her off her feet. His grip was more like a tug on a fish at the end of a line.

"Let me do this. You've got your hands full," said Remo, whistling for a cab. She wouldn't leave the briefcase. She shot him a deadly look.

"Never a cab when you need one," said Remo. He saw Stone. He had spotted him before. That was what held him up a fraction. He had to know where her death was coming from, so he could do something about it.

"Thanks for your help," said Major Fleming, pulling on the briefcase, "but I think I'll walk."

The car driven by the man with the shiny mouth pulled out from the curb to help. Without letting go of the briefcase, Remo stepped in front of a cab. He opened the door. He guided Major Fleming in, briefcase first. There was a minor problem. A passenger was already in the cab. Remo removed the problem. The cab driver didn't want to move. Remo gave the cabbie two things to encourage him to take the fare. A very nice ten-dollar bill and an intense finger pressure which crumbled the cabbie's change machine over the cabbie's lap. The driver pulled away, taking Major Fleming with him. Cars were honking as Remo assured the former passenger that he would get him a ride. Just wait in the middle of the street. The former passenger just spit and walked away. Remo dodged the saliva.

He also stepped in front of the car driven by the diamond-toothed man. He was trying to follow the cab.

"Got a problem, buddy?" Remo said to the man with the tooth, the man he had identified as Stone by description. After all, a diamond tooth was not exactly a hard thing to spot even in New York City.

Remo could sense the tense anger in Stone behind the wheel. He felt Stone about to step on the accelerator. He did not see the feet. He did not have to. It was all over the man's body. Strange, thought Remo, how when someone moves a foot, his shoulder lowers also. Most people did not realize how many parts of the body they used in each movement, or even how they breathed.

At the moment Remo realized he was thinking about his breath, at the instant he was about to be run over, he understood that everything was going to work. He was not thinking about trying not to be killed. He was the best of all things in this noisy New York City street, with the man about to drive a car through him, a traffic policeman strolling toward him to see what was wrong, and McCleary due to exit in a moment. He was beyond "good." He was correct. He was sure as sunrise, and cool as water. He was Sinanju, he was sure.

Before Stone could move, Remo moved. He was at the window of the car.

"Am I keeping you?" said Remo.

"Get out of the way," said Stone.

"You go wherever you want, sweetheart, just leave your throat with me," said Remo pleasantly. His hands cupped Stone's Adam's apple. He would not tear it out. However, if Stone wanted to start the car and leave it with Remo, that was Stone's business. Stone did not decide to leave.

"And don't honk. That will give the impression New Yorkers don't have manners," said Remo. He glanced down the street. Major Fleming's cab was on its way. Stone was trying to breathe. Remo knew this because the mouth was open. He stared at the tooth.

"Jeez. Who's your dentist? Tiffany's?"

Finally the cab was out of sight, the traffic cop had arrived to see what was holding up everything and, best of all, McCleary was moving out of the auditor general's office.

Done. Remo released Stone and gave McCleary a little nod. McCleary did not return it. McCleary was thinking, I am going to have to tell him about those little nods. A pro would pick that up.

Stone rubbed his neck with his left hand. With his right, he pressed the little rubber ball that clicked the camera in the lapel. He had seen the nod.

Remo returned to his training house, proud of himself for exactly three seconds.

McCleary was waiting. He explained in front of Chiun that Remo should never give an acknowledgment when they were not supposed to be working together. McCleary would take care of any acknowledgment if it were necessary.

Chiun, of course, did not understand a word of what McCleary was saying. He never quite understood why these people were keeping so much secret. Had Remo failed at a target?

No, McCleary said. Remo had not failed.

Then the enemy of the glorious Emperor Smith was dead.

No, said McCleary, the enemy was not dead. Today's assignment was not to kill someone. It was to protect someone.

"The greatest protection a man has is a dead enemy," said Chiun.

"They are not enemies so to speak," said McCleary. "But other than the nod, you did fine, laddie. That Fleming is some piece of work, isn't she?"

Chiun decided to keep quiet. There was an emperor who claimed he was not an emperor, nor did he want to be. That emperor wanted an assassin, but not for enemies. And the conversation had abruptly turned to the external form of a woman.

Chiun watched Remo closely. He obviously didn't think this was insane. He continued to talk about the woman. And it was not a code, Chiun determined quickly. There had been a woman in an elevator.

"Your training is good," said McCleary finally. "First mission passed almost perfectly."

"Thank you," said Remo.

There it was again. Almost perfectly. And Remo was thanking him for something. McCleary was waiting for Chiun to say something. What should he do at this moment with these whites? Talk about the attributes of his first wife?

"Good training," said McCleary again.

Chiun looked to Remo. Remo seemed happy.

"The assassination was correct?" asked Chiun.

"There was no killing," said the American McCleary.

"The person was almost dead. You delivered a head cold instead of a blow?"

"No. No. No kill," said McCleary. And he was happy with almost perfect and Remo was happy with almost perfect. Chiun decided to make some rice.

"A tribute to you and the House of Sinanju," said McCleary when he left.

"Of course," said Chiun. Remo couldn't explain it any better. He rambled on about the country, and the country's needs, about his pride in the country, and his love of the country.

Of course, he could not explain what the country had ever taught him, or done for him, he just kept saying how wonderful this country was, Chiun noticed.

And then Remo said:

"You know. Out there today, for the first time, I realized I was Sinanju, little father."

"Don't ever call me little father. I am not your father," said Chiun.

"I am sorry," said Remo. "It just came out."

"I am not your father. I am the Master of Sinanju, contracted to your Emperor Smith. Do not call me father."

"All right."

"Never call me father."

"I heard you. What's your problem?"

"I have no son."

"All right," said Remo. He had never seen Chiun so disturbed.

"And you are not Sinanju."

"Well, I felt it. I felt what you gave me."

"You are not Sinanju. You are not my son."

"Okay."

Chiun was quiet a moment. He looked at the boiling water and then back to Remo.

Finally he said:

"You must work on heights."

"Okay," said Remo.

"Heights are a thing that must be known by you."

"I understand."

"You are your own father, Remo."

"I understand. But I did know Sinanju out there in a New York City street with someone who was ready to drive a car into me. I knew that. I never knew my father or my mother, or half the things that went on in my life, but Chiun, Master of Sinanju, I knew out there at that moment, I was Sinanju."

"How, insolent pale piece of a pig's ear, did you know that?"

"Because when I thought the man might be killing me, I wasn't thinking about dying. I was thinking about breathing and movements and almost anything else in the world."

Chiun did not answer because he knew Remo was right. But while he was at that moment Sinanju, Sinanju was not his. It could leave him when he needed it most to survive, and then of course, all would be wasted. Remo would die.

Chiun thought of the promise made easily to Smith in secret, a promise that would not be easy now. He tried to explain to Remo what a professional assassin was, what Sinanju was in regards to the village.

Once upon a time, Sinanju was so poor, babies could not be fed and had to be put under the waters of the cold West Korea Bay. It was this poverty that led the Masters of Sinanju to give their services to the rich to feed the village. With each generation, more was learned. The genius of one Master could be built on by the next until they discovered the true powers of man, which they were.

"I know that," said Remo. "What are you getting at?"

"Every Master of Sinanju, if he fails to perform for the proper tribute, actually murders the babies of the village. So that we do not have choices sometimes."

"I still don't understand."

"We will work on heights," said Chiun to the man who had the glint of the stars in his eyes even though he was white. "We must conquer that."

"I don't know you at all, Chiun," said Remo. "And I will tell you something else. I don't want to know you."

"Good," said Chiun.

"Good," said Remo.

And that night they ate alone in silence.

Wilson had not failed. He had turned a setback into what could be the final breakthrough against "them," that hidden adversary who was getting less hidden by the moment.

"I think they're all here," said Wilson, throwing down three photographs onto Grove's desk, right next to the model of the Strider antiship torpedo, a unique device that could eliminate an entire convoy by homing in on the ship's munitions magazines. The Strider looked like an oblong silver sausage, with a slightly larger tip. The joke in Grove Industries was that the single women might be stealing the models to take home for private use. But it was not such a joke.

George Grove understood that if you could make a weapon a symbolic large male organ, without knowing it both Congress and the military would want the biggest ones they could buy.

The psychology department had come up with that one, and it had worked. The Russians responded without ever realizing what they were competing about. They built bigger ones.

One general once said over a minuscule difference, "Those Russians have us by six inches. Six crucial inches."

An Israeli general, committing his country to financial ruin, said his people needed the biggest ones around. An Arab sheik responded by saying he would drain all the oil from his country to assure that he, not the Jews, had the big ones.

He blamed American financial aid to Israel for the imbalance.

Many antiwar groups protested military aid and military expenditures by marching with placards demanding, "America; cut it off now."

The one thing Grove Industries would never acknowledge publicly was the subliminal message of many of their weapons designs.

The three photographs fell next to the model of the Strider.

"Wilson. I think you've done it. You couldn't have done better," said Grove. "May you miss like this all the time."

There, right before him, was the connection to all their recent troubles. The phony IRS investigator was now an equally phony bird colonel. And nodding to him was a man who had that very day prevented Stone from eliminating the problem of Major Rayner Fleming.

"This is it," said Wilson. "Here they are. Here is the reason for the mislead. Here are the reasons for our problems. They saved that bitch from being committed by General Watson to the funny farm, and then they saved her from elimination for good."

"There they are," said Grove.

"If they use a computer, and they do, we'll nail their headquarters within days. Days, George. Days. We've got the greatest technological resources of all time at our disposal. I hate to get overconfident, but we have it nailed. This is what we've been waiting for."

"Not overconfident at all, Wilson," said Grove. "But why did you fail?"

"It was a first time for Stone. He never missed before. There won't be a second," said Wilson.

"Who's this one?" asked Grove, pointing to the picture of a man smiling at a car windshield.

"That one is very interesting. No fingerprints anywhere. No recognition anywhere. The man might as well be dead."

"See to it."

"I have," said Wilson. "I couldn't deny Stone now. I'm doing a blanket on New York City. If that man moves within the city, we are going to spot him. And when we spot him . . ."

"Stone," said Grove.

"Almost as a favor to him," said Wilson.

If Remo were Sinanju, he would not labor his breathing. If Remo were Sinanju, he would not ask so many questions. If Remo were Sinanju, both he and Chiun would be at the top by now.

Thus spoke Chiun, who had been more critical than ever all morning. Remo had lost count of the stories they had climbed on the narrow metal stairs leading up to the shafts of light above them. All he knew was that it was up, and he didn't like up, because up meant high.

"I'd rather have the sex lessons. I mean how can you do a Korean courtship dance in an elevator? I failed in an elevator," said Remo. It felt like they were climbing forever.

"Do you ask me about the inner line stroke? No. Do you ask me about the scorpion defense? No. Do you ask me about the seven traditions and the ninety-nine steps of purity? No. Food and sex. Food and sex. This is what I have to deal with."

"How high are we now?"

"Almost perfect. Pretty good," said Chiun angrily. Stupid questions demanded similar answers.

When they were at the correct height, Chiun stopped. Light flooded in from a curve of windows above a narrow platform. New York City and its harbor spread out before them. On all sides there was water, no matter where they looked many stories below them.

The curves and drops were the closest things in this area to the training mountains outside of Sinanju. This was a large statue presented to the Americans by the French. There was only one problem. It was undergoing repairs and scaffolding abounded on its side.

"Don't hold on to the scaffolding," said Chiun. "You are not supposed to use your hands. It doesn't do you any good to hold on to scaffolding with your hands."

"Other than to keep me alive," said Remo.

"What a wonderful way to waste all my effort. Think about life and death at a time like this," said Chiun, and then beseeching the heavens, asked the forces of the universe where he had gone wrong in so mistraining this white.

That done, he ushered Remo outside to the little catwalk. Chiun himself would not descend the face and robes with Remo. He would observe from the bottom, making sure Remo, of course, did not use hands. A small elevator had just reached the crown, riding up along the scaffolding. Chiun passed three hardhat workers coming out of the elevator, and descended. This left Remo alone on the edge of the scaffolding, trying not to think of falling, of death, of that great distance way down there where if he landed, his body would be a bag of crushed bones.

It was very high, and he was very unsure. He grabbed the cold bar of the scaffolding for balance. He couldn't even stand. He knew now what Chiun had said about him having Sinanju was true. It was gone. He didn't have it. He would never have it.

Okay, fine. As long as he could get out of here, down by the elevator.

The three hardhat boomers made the scaffolding jiggle.

"Take it easy, will ya, fellas?" said Remo. Heights didn't bother them. Well, that was them. Remo wasn't them. And he wasn't Sinanju. He was getting down to the ground.

If Remo were not so scared he would have noticed the glint of the sun down below. He might have seen the man looking up at him with binoculars. He might have realized that the glint came from a diamond in a tooth.

But if he were not so scared, his balance would not be a question either, and standing many stories above the ground on repair scaffolding for a giant monument would not be a danger. The plank he stood on would have been more than enough, and the boomers in the hard hats, the men who worked heights, would not have bothered him. Their easy bounce along the plank would not have forced Remo to grab on to a scaffolding bar.

"Take it easy, fellas. Okay?" said Remo. They didn't have to jostle the scaffolding like that. Not everyone liked heights.

The boomers looked at each other and smiled. They all heard the request. They bounced harder.

"Hey, you guys crazy?" said Remo.

"What are you doing here?" asked a boomer. He looked like he was born fifty stories off the ground.

"We work here. Do you work here?" said another boomer.

"Authorized personnel only. We don't want any accidents," said another.

"Or suicides," said the first. The plank moved dangerously.

"Okay. So I'm going down. Now. Down. Me. Just stop that, okay?" said Remo, trying to get across the plank. He would not walk unless he was holding on to one scaffolding bar before releasing the other.

"Yeah," said the first boomer. "You're on your way down, all right. The short way."

Remo felt the plank jangle as the boomer jogged down it toward him, his arms raised, trying to push him off. They may have been real boomers. He didn't know. But they were trying to kill him. And here, with his fear out of control, they were going to succeed. He saw a crossbar on the scaffolding below.

With feet like lead, and hands like ice cubes, Remo dove for it. The hands held, barely. The body felt like a bag of bricks. It swayed. He clutched the bar as though trying to tear off his skin. But he was safe.

Until all three of the boomers easily jumped down to his level, jumped with the grace of acrobats, acrobats chasing the bag of bricks.

Remo reached out for another strut, but the fear tightened his body and the hand missed. He was falling. But just for a second. Something stopped him. He was on the thumb, the great thumb. He looked up. He had been on the torch. He had fallen from the lady's torch to her thumb. The green copper flaked on his face and under his hands. He could taste the sharp odor. His arms and legs wide over the thumb, he tried not to scrape off the outer layer of copper. And he tried not to look down. He had one great wish. Never to leave this thumb, this safe place, his home, his destiny, everything. He loved this copper thumb. He loved it so much, he didn't even want to look away from it. He wanted to stay there on the thumb, and be nowhere else. His thumb. His place. His cheek very close to the copper, hugging it.

And then Remo heard the scraping. It was right above his head on the thumb. Something tapped his hands, then scraped them. Remo had to look up. The boomers had one of the pole scrapers used for chipping the flaked copper away from the statue. They were scraping him off his thumb. He crawled back away from the thing that threatened to remove him from his thumb.

He felt the copper come up quickly to his face, then slip away from above him, hundred-year-old weathered copper coming up in a funnel at his mouth. He was sliding. He was sliding down the arm of the Statue of Liberty, down the forearm, the bicep, into the robes seen by millions arriving in America. Remo's view was that of a man who was leaving the country, and the earth, forever.

And then he was free of the copper, falling, falling free until he cracked into one bar, several bars, many bars . . . he was falling through scaffolding. And then the fall stopped. Remo was still grabbing, but he had landed on another platform. Painfully, expecting an arm or a leg to suddenly scream at him that it was broken, Remo made his way back up, careful not to look at the ground.

But at the last few steps, scaffolding had been removed. And beneath him was the chasm. He thought of them getting away, and he thought, good. He would be alive.

He felt his breath come strong, breath that almost left. And he drew it in, breathed like he had been taught, breathed until he was breathing correctly.

He brushed the copper off his clothes, without any pressure on the platform, moved across to the statue on the fine day whose brightness hid the stars that would show again that night.

He could have taken the elevator. But elevators were slow. And now, he had no intention of letting them get away, as he let his fingertips lightly brush the patina of the skin of the flaky copper, sensing the very salt that had bathed it these many years, feeling the air, and the mass of the statue and the sea, and the movement, the unity of the movement, the correctness of moving down a great height.

Stone received his men at the base of the statue, sparing any words of recognition. They would not be down here if they had not succeeded. It had been a classic move. If a man seemed comfortable in one area, such as on a city street, go at him at another. Such as on the Statue of Liberty.

The plan had one flaw. Stone saw that in an instant. The man had survived. He was on the ground, coming out from behind the base of the statue, coming at the boomers with blood in his eyes.

One of Stone's men in the boomer's hard hat went for his pistol.

"Do him," said Stone.

On the other side of the statue, Chiun heard a shot. He had watched Remo and made observations for future reference. It had taken Remo too long to realize he was being attacked, but that was not the problem; it was only a symptom of the problem. The problem was what he had come here to solve. Fear of heights. A shot rang out from the other side of the statue, not loudly. Pistols were hardly loud surrounded by so much water, where sound waves tended to dissipate.

Chiun, who had been helping a family take pictures, handed back the camera and went to see about the shot. Remo would be there. There were things he needed to learn about fear, if he hadn't learned them already. Even if he had learned by now, it should not have taken so long.

There were lots of things to tell him. Chiun moved happily toward the pistol shot.

The way to dodge a bullet of course was not to dodge a bullet. Instead, one dodged the very slow body sending the bullet, aiming the bullet. And of course this man's body gave much heavier signals than Chiun's. It was almost laughably easy. But Remo did not want this man right now.

He wanted that man with the diamond in the tooth. Remo skimmed across a trough of wet cement, rounded the corner of the statue, and saw Stone riding away in a small motorboat. The boat made good speed on the choppy waves.

Remo thought about the water. Was it like wet sand? Could he move across it? The man with the diamond tooth was getting away, and Remo burned in his belly.

The anger was just as wrong as the fear. Because of it, he did not see another boomer, not the one who foolishly tried to follow him across wet cement and got stuck for his trouble, aim a pistol at the back of his head.

Bullets could not be dodged when one was unaware of the person firing. The bullet was well set for Remo's brain and would have reached its mark had it not been for the long fingernail shooting out so quickly the human eye could not spot it. It paralyzed the boomer and sent him spinning. And still Remo didn't turn around.

He didn't turn around when the force of Chiun's thrust on the boomer impaled him on rusting wires.

He didn't turn around to notice the man with the gun, stuck in the cement. He didn't turn around of course to notice Chiun. He stood there trembling with his hatred, this after all these months of Chiun's perfect training.

Was this what Chiun deserved? Was this his return for the awesome magnificence he had cast before the meat eater, the man who would want to copulate with a woman just because she was ravishing, not even caring whether she breathed correctly?

But that was all right, Chiun was used to these things. And he had found what he had come around the statue to find. Once again, another injustice had been visited upon perhaps the most decent and giving person Chiun had ever known. Himself.

Chiun turned away from this, and content that the order of the world had been reaffirmed, walked over to some young boys fishing to tell them that a good fisherman does not use a hook or a rod, or string. They, of course, were white and answered him with insolence.

"How can you fish without hooks and line?" they said, without calling him "gracious one" even once.

But he was not paid to teach them, so he ignored their question. Undoubtedly they would grow up adding themselves to the rubble of this civilization into which Remo fit so well.

Remo arrived with sweat on his body and breathing hard, even as the death rattle on his first exercise could be heard by the trained ear on the other side of the statue. What an awful beginning.

"Well, it worked," said Remo. "Most of the time it was correct."

"Go fish with a hook and a line," said Chiun.

"Listen, I almost got killed up there," said Remo.

"Yes," said Chiun, feeling the frustration of it all. "Disgraceful. You breathe hard. You perspire, and you show anger. And you show fear. You are a shame to the breath I taught you to take."

"I am happy to be alive," said Remo.

"You should be," said Chiun. And he refused to say another word all the way back to the mainland.

The problems that afternoon were just beginning for Smith and McCleary, however. And it was Remo who was going to tell them about it, only to find out about the horrible secret those two men shared. And the one Chiun had been struggling with, the one he had learned from the devious Harold W. Smith. It would explain to Remo why Chiun could never let him call the man "little father."

It would explain why Chiun had to tell him about an assassin's first loyalty. It would be something that would break Remo's heart. But orphans were used to that.

13

The protection for the HARP system financial spread sheets was working again.

"Look at this," said Smith. McCleary peered at the screen. Although he did not know computers, he could read. Access was denied.

McCleary thought of another access denied, one that he kept trying to push out of his mind. That very afternoon he had been denied an apartment because he was black. It was against the law to do so, illegal in one of the few countries that had such a law, but people did it nevertheless.

And here he was risking his life for a country that didn't let him live where he wanted because of the color of his skin. It made it all very hard, and took the edge off his concentration.

"Is that the access I got by physically infiltrating Grove Industries?"

"Right. Once they believed you were an Internal Revenue agent, they had to show you their books, which were of course on their computer. You got the path codes for getting into HARP which also protected the original AR-60 from

Army audit. That's what we were looking at first. But look at what's going on here."

McCleary took in a sequence of meaningless numbers. "Right," he said. He remembered the landlady's face. It showed such pain. You always knew when they were lying because they showed pain at not having an apartment available. That was the dead giveaway. Otherwise, it would just be another apartment already rented, a simple sorry and good-bye.

When they said no because you were black, there was that special pain to the face, the lengthy explanation of who had just rented the apartment, all delivered at top speed.

Sometimes he would stand there and let them squirm. But Con McCleary didn't enjoy it. He knew what it was all about, and sometimes it made him feel so tired, tired of everything. Tired of caring. Tired of trying. Tired of being an American.

But he was an American. He knew how bad Africa was. Maybe white liberal professors and African scholars had to keep afloat some myths of value either for their jobs or their good intentions, but he knew it was a garbage pit, from Tripoli to Cape Town. And Asia treated all human life with the compassion one normally bestowed on grass seed.

The problem for Con McCleary was that America was home. He wouldn't trade a cold beer at an American bar for all the champagne in Paris. He liked fried chicken, beer and baseball. If he read a book, chances were it was history, and usually American history. He did his job because he was an American. His father worked in the post office and his grandfather worked on the trains, and McCleary saved the whole damned thing for people who wouldn't rent him living space.

Smitty, on the other hand, had been part of this country since before it was a country, McCleary knew. Sometimes he wondered if that made that much difference. Sometimes he wanted to ask. But you didn't ask Harold W. Smith those sorts of questions. You didn't ask him personal things or tell him personal things. You watched computer screens and talked about economic access.

"Now here is protection for America's most sensitive protection satellite, so new it hasn't been orbited, so sensitive that they may have HARP II in space before they ever need HARP I. Now what is maximum protect?"

"What I see there, I guess. I don't know. Get to the point, Smitty," said McCleary.

"The financial records."

"I got access to them for us."

"You did, but you don't know the higher levels of these things."

"And I never will, happily," said McCleary.

"When something is absolutely most important, maximum, all the other protection devices work to scrutinize it. It's like a night watchman. He doesn't check the fence to see if it is still there, he checks the locks on the doors to the room where the money is kept. What they have done is to devote their maximum protection to their financial records. Why?"

"They're white," said McCleary.

"Be serious," said Smith. "Logic would dictate that the HARP I would have its maximum protect on its technological secrets, how one builds one of these things or gets around one of these things. But these people have put it on the books. Costs. Why?"

A red light flashed on the corner of the screen. Someone was entering the outer office. The cameras replaced the computer readout with an image of the intruder. The face was hard, and angry.

"He's not supposed to come here unless we tell him," said Smith. It was Remo.

"Well, he's here," said McCleary. "And he looks pissed. I would be very careful with that one. He is not the same guy we fished out of the river. Remo Williams is something else entirely."

"But Chiun's reports?" asked Smith.

"Hey, those people, Smitty, are them. Them don't think like us. And this boy we shanghaied may be becoming one of them, so don't play street games like this was the community."

"Is there a purpose to that sudden black talk?" asked Smith.

"To save our asses. We got what we want, I think. But I don't think we know what we got, and that sonuvabitch Remo is getting better. I saw him dodge bullets. And he hasn't gotten worse since then."

Remo entered on a tear.

He did not ask permission to enter. He did not say hello. He informed them they were all going to straighten something out. McCleary was glad he had warned Smith.

Remo was covered by flaky green stuff. His face was cut, his dark eyes burned.

"I just spent the morning being chased around the Statue of Liberty by a bunch of goons."

"What were you doing on the statue?" asked Smith.

"That's not the point. What were the guys who were trying to kill me doing on the Statue of

Liberty? You're supposed to be plugged into the universe and you can't warn me when someone is staging a hit? I thought we were supposed to go after them. They were coming after me."

"Who?" asked McCleary.

"Our friend with the Tiffany tooth," said Remo. "Who gave me away to him? I'm supposed to be secret. I'm supposed to be the man who doesn't exist for the organization that doesn't exist. What was that thing in the police car and the plastic surgery for if you assholes are going to list me in the phone book or something?"

Smith and McCleary looked at each other. McCleary's mouth opened. Smith became even paler. He swallowed hard. His voice jerked with fear under control, like a string on a violin stretched too taut.

"What do you think?" Smith asked. But he did not ask it of Remo.

"I think we are very close to buying the farm," said McCleary.

"Not yet," said Smith.

"If he's on to Remo, then he's on to us. We've got a problem," said McCleary.

"Damned right you do. Someone tried to kill me," said Remo.

"Let's take him out before he gets closer?" asked McCleary. His voice almost begged.

Smith shook his head. "No. Not yet. We don't know what it means absolutely for sure."

"It means some guy tried to kill me. If you know where he is, let me at him. I'll do it. I don't need you people to tell me how to be correct with a target. Hell, you had tunafish with oily mayonnaise for lunch, Smith, and you had fried chicken for the last three days, McCleary."

Smith turned to Remo, and with all the authority he naturally had felt because of the rightness of his cause, he said quite coldly:

"Remo, CURE is not interested in your personal problems."

"Well, cure sucks, whatever cure is."

"Exactly what it says," said Smith. "The three of us in this room are CURE. A cure for the crime and lawlessness that threaten to swamp this country and ultimately make it ungovernable."

"I knew we were doing something like that. You told me."

"Yes, but did we tell you that if it became known we exist, it would be an admission by our government that the whole kit and caboodle does not and cannot work? That our laws don't work?"

"What are you getting at?"

"We created a killer arm that does not exist for an organization that does not exist. You learned to fight without weapons that would leave a trace. You are our only real killer arm. Why?"

"Because I am beautiful. What are you getting at?"

"We cannot be known to exist or everything we are fighting for goes. America becomes just another little police state above its own laws like any third-world country," said Smith.

"A man named Grove has to have discovered your existence to send the man with the diamond tooth. If he knows about you, he may know about us."

"He didn't try to kill you," said Remo. "You're afraid now. Am I the only one who's supposed to be shot at?"

"I will not be shot at," said Smith. "If we are discovered, every file in our computers automatically self-destructs. And so do we. All of us. I have a pill. It is fast. It is painless. It is final."

"Harold W. Smith, research analyst, will be found with a suicide note," said McCleary, "and Con McCleary will be found with his brains blown out. Niggers with bullets in their heads are not uncommon in this great land of ours. No one will ask any questions about me. A black man can always find a place somewhere if it is beneath the ground."

"Where does that leave me?" asked Remo.

"Well, you would be a bit much for us to kill now. Your abilities far surpass ours, from what McCleary tells me," said Smith.

"So?"

"So there is only one man on earth equipped to kill you."

"No," said Remo. All the secrets were out. He didn't care what else they said. It couldn't be true. Chiun wouldn't kill him. Most of the Master's complaining was only proof of how much Chiun cared. Remo was sure of that. He was so sure that the complaining didn't bother him anymore. He was certain of it. They were wrong.

The two of them worked out a plan while Remo thought of what he would say to Chiun. McCleary and Remo would hit the security-tight HARP manufacturing complex in West Virginia. HARP had to be the key to Grove Industries and if they could crack HARP, they could crack Grove. Then George Grove's personal killer network could be eliminated, and CURE and all of them would go on.

When they asked Remo if he understood, he said yes. He would have said yes to anything. But first he had to speak to Chiun.

Chiun had learned how to tape the daytime

soap operas so he could have dramas from all three networks played at his leisure. He now followed all of them daily and talked about the characters as though they were real people.

He was watching one of the soaps when Remo arrived back at the training house. Seeing him more absorbed in the drama than apparently he was in Remo's life, Remo thought a moment. Maybe what Smith said was so. He started to speak. Then he decided not to. Then he decided to say something. Then he decided not to.

He stood there, making no sounds audible to normal people.

"You want to say something?" said Chiun.

"Yeah," said Remo. "You know, I heard something, not that I believe it. You know. I don't believe everything people say. I know what you've given me, and I know you wouldn't just throw that away, right?"

"The answer is yes, Remo. I am a Master of Sinanju. My first loyalty is to the village. I would kill you. It is in the contract."

As for breathing, Remo didn't care to. But he noticed he had stopped, just stopped. His mouth was open, his feet were frozen to the floor. There wasn't anything left to say. Chiun had said it all. And Remo had wanted to call the man "little father."

Well, he didn't have any father he ever knew of, and this man wasn't one either. He had the nuns at the orphanage, who used to send him Christmas cards every year until a change of address threw them off his trail. He had his football coach, who remembered him for two years as the best middle linebacker he had ever seen until he got someone who made second-string all-American.

And Remo had himself. He had himself, and he had his job, and he had what he knew how to do, and he packed a little bag and left the training house alone.

He did not see the Master of Sinanju turn off the television set. He could not of course see the Master of Sinanju remember his own son lost in the heights.

And he did not hear the sound come from Chiun's throat.

"Ah," said Chiun, but it held no satisfaction. It was as empty as the far side of the universe where stars did not reflect the sun.

"Nothing is bothering me," said Remo, as their car traversed the bleak hills of West Virginia, heading on a road toward a place far away called Parkersburg. They were going beyond Parkersburg.

Remo didn't see whether there would be much difference where they went. All across the country, there were plenty of run-down roadside bars that looked as though they were being held together by their neon signs that advertised beer. The West Virginia ones were only marginally different. They didn't have the signs.

"You haven't talked to me since New York. What's bothering you?"

"Nothing. I told you nothing is bothering me," said Remo. "Let's do the job and get out of here. You talk a lot. All right? Don't talk so much."

"I didn't say a word all through Pennsylvania, laddie. What's bothering you?"

"I remember. It was peaceful all the way through Pennsylvania," said Remo. "Yeah, something is bothering me. I don't have a father, that's bothering me. I don't have a mother. That's bothering me, too."

"You just found that out, Remo?"

"You and Smith know more about me than I do, probably."

"We never found out who your parents were, if that's what you're asking, Remo," said McCleary. He drove easily, just enough speed to get there, yet not enough to attract attention from a traffic policeman, not that they had seen a policeman on the road since they entered the state. The shacks and roadside bars, and advertisements for chewing tobacco, were suddenly replaced by a large ugly chemical factory, lit like a stadium in hell, with smoke wafting through the harsh floodlights. Chain-link fence and warnings surrounded its base. The whole factory was set on a river. This was the plant just south of Grove Industries. It was actually a Grove subsidiary, acting almost as an outpost. The car would be tracked the minute it passed this plant. They were coming up against the best technology in the world; America's own. Fortunately, Smitty had known it was there. The plant itself was not quite as well-protected as the accounting for HARP.

As of this point, both of them knew anything they said in the car could be heard by the monitors situated in the Grove complex ahead. Ironically, from this point on, they could say anything personal they wished but nothing about business. McCleary nodded to the factory. They had discussed this before. Remo nodded back. He understood.

"I used to imagine my father would teach me things if I had one. Really. I was never really good at anything in my life. I was never the best. And I always thought that if I had a father, he would have taught me how to be the best. I used to think things like that," said Remo. "I did."

"And you thought he was your father?"

"I did."

"Until you found out he had a contractual obligation to us instead of you."

"Well, I think you, he, and the other guy are all . . ." said Remo. He couldn't get the words out. He waited a few moments until the rage subsided. And then simply added:

"Enjoy yourself. I quit."

"Wait a minute, laddie. Not now," said McCleary.

"I could live with what you did to me at the beginning. I accepted that. But what the old man told me back there—what you arranged with him—I just don't think the whole country is worth it. That's what I think. That's what's bothering me. That's what I have been thinking about."

"This country is worth a lot, Remo. I don't think you know enough of the world to know how blessed this country is."

"You had a father and mother, laddie," said Remo, imitating McCleary. "When you have parents, you have a piece of this country. When you don't have a father you don't have nothing. It's your country, laddie. Not mine," said Remo. "That's what I'm feeling."

The factory ended along the road, and of course, the shabby bars began again.

"You see those bars?" asked McCleary.

"How can I miss 'em? The whole state is loaded with them. What do they have? Some sort of zoning ordinance that prohibits the number of homes you can build without a cheap roadside bar to service them?"

"I probably could not walk out alive from most of those bars, because of the color of my skin.

When I go to small towns I don't know if I can find a place to sleep because of the color of my skin. And more times than not, the places I want to live, I can't live. . . ."

"Those bars?" said Remo, nodding to the side of the road.

"Any of them practically. I wouldn't go in unless I was ready to shoot my way out."

"Stop the car."

"We have a schedule."

"Stop the car," said Remo. "You and I are going to have a beer."

McCleary felt Remo's foot work its way to the brake. He couldn't kick the leg away.

"We'll have a beer later," said McCleary.

"Now," said Remo.

"I don't want a beer that much. When we're . . . To hell with it." Somehow Remo had gotten his feet and hands on the wheel and pedal in such a way that McCleary couldn't pry them off. He wasn't driving the car anymore.

McCleary pulled the car over to the first brightly lit sign as an alternative to coming to a halt in the middle of the road.

"We'll get a couple of bottles to go," said McCleary as they entered the din and darkness of a bar that smelled like an armpit gone sour. As McCleary had thought, there wasn't a black face in the room. Someone pointed that out.

Another person announced loudly that the bar didn't serve baboons. Even in the dim light McCleary could make out just what clientele this bar did serve—big persons. Some of them had their sleeves cut off to make room for very big biceps. One of them offered to show his girlfriend "what the insides of a nigger look like on a barroom floor."

And then brotherhood came to this little roadside tavern on the West Virginia byway. Remo noticed the bar had spills on it. So he wiped them off. He wiped off every little puddle of beer and every last nutshell so that it was neat. He did this with the two largest men in the bar.

And since they were now dirty rags he tossed them through the front windows.

Everyone was so impressed with Remo's tidiness that they came to admire his handiwork on the bar. A man with a hunting knife was the first to look. He was so impressed he left the imprint of his skull and face on the glossy surface, then collapsed on the floor.

The two largest men quivered in the little gravel space used for a parking lot. There wasn't one person who interfered with the well-dressed black man's drinking. In fact, several offered to buy him drinks but he refused.

"Do you feel better now?" said McCleary, checking his watch. They hadn't lost much time, but they had lost time.

"Yeah," said Remo. "Do you?"

"Do you think I take pleasure in watching you abuse poor ignorant people who don't know any better?"

"Sure," said Remo.

"I did, damn me. I did, laddie," said McCleary, with a big laugh from the belly. "I loved it. I wish I could do something like that about your father problem."

"To hell with it. I got work."

"I could get to like you, laddie," said McCleary. "But I won't."

And both of them understood that one might be called upon to kill the other in an emergency.

"You already do, asshole," said Remo.

"You didn't take a beer back there."

"My system doesn't use alcohol. There is no purpose to it."

"You used to drink a lot."

"I used to eat for taste too," said Remo. And McCleary understood that as American as Remo appeared, there was something else going on in him that McCleary would never fathom.

The signs for Grove appeared as warnings: "Roads Ahead Impassable," then "Private Property." Only when they had reached the high wire gates did they see the signs marked with the skull and crossbones indicating danger.

They, like those in every vehicle on that dismal stretch of road, had been monitored for several miles back. They parked the car at a small lot near a guardhouse, showing proper identification.

They could have used those papers to get into the plant, but such was the sophistication of the HARP defenses that identification, unless verified personally by someone inside who knew them, would be invalid within an hour. And more important, according to what Smith could make out, the defenses of the HARP complex were such that it was harder to get out than to get in.

What they had to try to do was avoid the entire checking system, stay out of the Grove personnel-identification machine. The plan was simple. Cut their way in under a fence, commando style. Remo and McCleary walked back down the road, then suddenly dropped, lying there quiet in the frosty grass and chill night air, waiting to see if anyone noticed. And when no one had, McCleary eased a wire cutter up in front of him, and clipped. The wire hissed and sparked. It was electrified. McCleary grabbed it with his left hand. The left hand smoked and sputtered. But it did not release the wire.

"Did Chiun teach you that?" whispered Remo. "How do you do that? I can't do that."

"You lose your hand to an antipersonnel mine in Nam and you replace it with an artificial one."

So McCleary had one hand. That explained his talk about leaving only one handprint wherever he went. McCleary said it tended to confuse people, but not as much as he liked. Now Remo understood.

Inside the fence, fifty yards of gravel and grass surrounded a four-story building. Pools of light from shaded overhead bulbs at regular intervals illuminated the red-brick masonry and ironwork. It was an old factory.

Service trucks and crates littered a side road leading to a modern administration building farther back. No words were exchanged as the pair split. McCleary would meet Remo back at the opening. He headed for the administration building. Remo headed for the factory. Remo became part of the night. McCleary had to try to keep quiet on the balls of his feet. McCleary's nerves were taut. Remo's were correct. To him, this was not life and death; this was proper and improper.

Remo entered through a wood-frame window. The paint was new. The wood was old. Now here was the prototype of the most sophisticated electronics in America's arsenal, and it was housed in this old factory with wood-frame windows. Why?

It seemed odd to break into a place and not feel fear or anxiety. Remo noticed the change in himself but did not feel it. One did not use feelings for that at a time like this. It was dark. He sensed sounds throughout the building. He could almost hear Chiun expounding on the proper way to enter a castle. He just substituted factory. As for the target, he substituted the HARP prototype.

The factory was open inside, dark but for partial moonlight coming from skylights above. Catwalks surrounded the open space like a prison. The room smelled of old dust, and shoe polish and dogs. Probably watchdogs, thought Remo.

Remo heard the pads on the floor. He turned. Saw it. German shepherd. Teeth bared. Midair. At him.

And by him. Remo let it bite at air, and moved through the open space to the lower platform circling the inside of the factory. He took a skip-jump to the lower rail and lifted himself just as the dog got a mouthful of trouser. With that foot, he flicked it off with a turning toe into the neck. The blow landed solidly. Funny, thought Remo, the animals always do it right. And he remembered all that Chiun had said about animals, where they were right and man was wrong. Animals always believed in themselves.

Two more dogs padded well out into the center of the factory and joined the other. Remo thought he was safe from them for a moment until one leaped at a bar, and then the other joined him. It was a game of fetch. Grab the bar, and their weight lowered a ladder. Then they could fetch the man with their bare teeth.

They ran toward him. Remo leaped to the walkway above. And they ran upstairs to join him. As he moved higher, so did they until they all reached the roof. Remo was outside. It was five stories to the ground.

He thought about it. Mistake. A searing pain gripped his hand. A dog was on it, hanging on by its teeth. Another one got in behind him. And he was high on the roof. He slipped a hand under the jaws of the large dog and opened them, freeing his hand just as one of the others bowled into him, sending him to the edge, holding on to crumbling brick. He felt something below. There was a ledge. It was a window. He dropped to it. Little ugly screeching sounds came at his feet. Rats. He felt prickly clawing up his pants leg. Up his calf. At his knee. Still going. A rat in his pants. The dogs on the edge of the roof were about to jump down to get him, and Remo smashed in the window with his head and dove into the factory.

He landed correctly, letting the whole body dissipate the force of the landing and unzipping his fly to release the trapped intruder.

A large "Access Forbidden" sign hung over a doorway. Remo tested the door. It was good steel. As Chiun had said, the best iron gates always guard the king. And the king in this case was HARP. He pressured the handle into the lock and it snapped with the ease of a garter.

And then he was in the room. But he was not prepared for what he would see. Smith had drawn him a rough sketch of HARP in his office. But there it only looked like a cube.

This cube was eight feet on all sides, and hung from the ceiling. Each side was a burnished metal, and the moon played golden on its polish. It was beautiful. Remo thought of what had to be inside. All the knowledge of a technological age, the perfection of defense achievement. He heard a buzzing. It came from above the doorway. A motor. A small motor. It drove a thing with a round glass barrel. A camera. It stopped when it pointed at him. It could spot movement.

Remo remained still, but it was too late. The camera flashed a red light, and then the light moved across the floor and quickly up the wall.

The camera was aiming. The light hit HARP. The red glowed ugly, chasing the warm colors of the reflection of the move. And then in a blast of white light, HARP exploded and alarms went off.

Remo had triggered a self-destruct mechanism.

McCleary had just backed out of the door of the administration building. Everything had gone more smoothly than he could have hoped. Smith, in his usual brilliance, had pinpointed exactly what McCleary should get, and exactly where it should be, and there it was. McCleary had it; he had taken it exactly as Smith said he might be able to get it, and Remo over at the HARP prototype had blown up the building. Sirens were wailing and searchlights crisscrossing the whole place, and guards and dogs and guns made the whole place an inside of hell.

Con McCleary at that moment felt he could kill Remo. Wrong. He wanted to kill Remo. He didn't know if he could ever kill him again.

One thing could be said about the boy. He could move. While Con McCleary had to work at getting back to the meeting point by carefully ducking from crate to crate, following moving trucks, trying to pretend to be part of the guarding force, Remo just moved. He was waiting near the fence hole when McCleary got there exhausted.

"I think I blew it," said Remo.

"Don't worry. We got what we need, I think," said McCleary.

"We also got our escape cut off," said Remo. McCleary couldn't see what he was talking about. And then the searchlights blanketed the hole they cut, lighting it as though it were the infield of the Astrodome at night, and McCleary saw the guards run through the hole at them.

"C'mon," said McCleary. "Those bulldozers."

Remo ran to the bulldozer, and then realized that McCleary was still puffing along after him. A dog had gotten to his artificial arm and McCleary left the arm with the dog. Without it, McCleary ran crippled. The best he could manage was a lumbering, puffing, listing lunge.

Remo had the dozer running by the time McCleary got there.

"You got black man's feet," said Remo in revenge of his high-school years when blacks had outrun him and outplayed him, when the joke was if a player couldn't move fast, he had what was called the "white man's disease."

"Through the fence," said McCleary. Remo worked the gears. McCleary helped him. The bulldozer rattled and chugged, its treads crushing the gravel and scrub, moving forward. Remo helped McCleary jump off. The dozer chugged on into the electrified fence, setting off an explosion of light that would make a rock star envious.

They ran through the fence, and McCleary almost caught up to Remo, even with his sloppy gait, when his body jerked at the sound of a rifle bullet. Someone had gotten him in the back. McCleary went forward, too fast, faster than his legs, and he landed on the gravel.

Remo spun on the spot and turned back for McCleary. Another shot chipped stone at his feet. He couldn't sense the men firing in the confusion.

"Get out of here. Take this. Get it to home. Get it to home," said McCleary. He was pushing a cardboard package about half as long as a carton of cigarettes and twice as wide. "Get this to home. Go. Move it."

Remo grabbed the package. "Home" meant Smith. But he wasn't leaving without McCleary.

Then he saw the eyes roll back in McCleary's head, and the head hit the ground, and two more shots came too close, too close for someone who might already be dead. Two dead would do no one any good. Besides, that's what CURE was about anyway. You gave up your body for your country.

Only when he was sure Remo had gone did McCleary open his eyes. The bullet he'd taken had touched off a dull pain McCleary knew would get worse later. At that point, he did not know how much worse.

McCleary only found out how much pain he could truly endure when a doctor who found him at the Grove site began asking him questions about "home."

The doctor told him that the treatment might hurt. He kept asking if this was painful and that was painful as he poked a scalpel over McCleary's body, looking for places that hurt. And he found them with surgical skill.

"We picked up, albeit not too clearly, that you wanted to get something home. What is home? Where is home? Who are you?"

The man seemed to know when McCleary was faking passing out.

"Come now. We know you are with us. Who are you?"

The probing knife touched McCleary's left eye.

"Look. We have seen you as an investigator for the Internal Revenue Service. We have seen you as a bird colonel in New York and now we see you again, here at one of our factories. Who are you this time?" The voice was low and reasonable. McCleary could not make out the person in the dark. He felt a gouging near the eye.

"Are you really going to make me go through this?" came the voice.

McCleary smelled the sharp odor of hospital disinfectant. He realized there would be no rescue here. He was in a hospital. Any screams for help would be considered normal. They could call him hysterical and none of the nurses or doctors who weren't part of this group would come to his aid. No one would come to his aid; he was sure of that. He had set up Remo that way in the beginning. McCleary knew from experience that he wasn't getting out of here alive.

Even if he were in a friendly hospital he might not get out of here alive. He saw the support tubes holding his life this side of breathing going up from his nose and one good arm. There was that dullness of the body he knew had to precede death.

He felt something on his chest. The questioner had rested the scalpel there, as if it were a convenient table.

"Why don't you think about all the places this little knife can go, and all the things it can do. You think awhile and then I will come back. I will come back to either give you the warm comfort of a good narcotic, or the scalpel. And while you think, focus on who you are and where 'home' is, and what all this was about tonight. Would you do that for me?"

McCleary could make out the man's white coat, though he did not see the diamond in his mouth. Nor did he hear the conversation that went on outside his room of the Grove Hospital.

"You should have called me sooner, he's almost dead," said Stone.

"Well?" said Wilson. He hated West Virginia. Even the governors wore off-the-rack suits.

"I think he has enough life left in him to give us what we want," said Stone. "I am going to let his mind work against him for a little while. Then we will have it all."

"This is lucky. This does it. We have them now. They gave themselves to us on a silver platter."

"Unless of course they were after something here at the West Virginia plant."

"Well, whatever they got, we are going to get it back," said Wilson. "That is the beautiful part of that gift they have given us. We have them now. Do you think he's had enough time?"

"I think so," said Stone, and his smile glistened.

Even if he got the information, Stone had no intention of providing a narcotic. Not because he got any real delight from inflicting cruelty, but because a scalpel through the heart was the finest, most permanent narcotic of all. And of course, in a hospital, no one would notice.

Stone realized that something was wrong as soon as he entered the room. He did not hear the rhythmic rasp of labored breathing. He checked the life-support system—the phosphorous screens were sending out a steady signal. None of the jerks of life. Then he heard his foot squish in some liquid. He looked down. It was dark, reddish; and a tube poured silently into the puddle. Stone himself had attached the tube to the one good arm of the intruder. Now the arm hung over the bed, and in the puddle was the scalpel. He had cut the tube; severed the intravenous connection for the blood transfusion. When it was cut, the blood no longer flowed into the body, but out of it. Stone felt the chest. Nothing. He felt the wrist. Nothing. He checked the monitor. It was flat.

He wasn't going to get any information out of this man. He had escaped once and for all.

Later, in New York City, Harold W. Smith unraveled the mysteries surrounding HARP, and couldn't help giving George Grove just a little bit of admiration.

"I knew that son of a bitch was smart, but I didn't know he was this smart," said Smith. Remo had delivered McCleary's package.

14

Remo rubbed his hand where the dog had caught him back in the Grove HARP plant in West Virginia. Smith kept nodding at the computer screen. On the green background a white diagram appeared, delineating the outer container of HARP. Then its flight path developed, stretching a protecting web over the western world.

Remo did not mind the pain in his hand. He understood that that sort of pain meant that his body was curing itself. Remo minded very much that Smith was calling Grove "very smart." He minded very much that these people had killed McCleary. He had just gotten to like him in West Virginia.

He would never, he was sure, feel the same thing for this man and his computers. He was sure that being able to say something nice about the other guy had a great deal to do with the camaraderie that came of putting your guts on the line together. But Remo really couldn't convince himself that that was the case. Smith did have that pill in his pocket. He was going to kill himself if CURE were exposed. And that made Remo think of who would be killing him.

"Look here and see what that smart son of a bitch has done. Look," said Smith.

"I don't give a wind spit," said Remo.

"You should. Look at this. This explains it all. Our friend George Grove of Grove Industries has not only sucked billions from our taxpayers, our good friend George Grove has sent us out into this cold world without a protective stitch. Look at that."

Remo saw some numbers come on the screen. Then he saw a graph drawing of something going out into space. Then he saw some more numbers.

"Numbers," said Remo.

"America's roof," said Smith. "Our protection from the nuclear rain."

"What?" said Remo. The hand was better.

"It doesn't exist."

"No. I saw it in West Virginia. It was beautiful. Like sculpture. It blew up in my face."

"What you saw was a fake. Window dressing. And before you got close enough to figure that out, it self-destructed. Brilliant."

"So Grove is just another crook."

"I wish that were true," said Smith. "You see the reason he surrounded HARP I with so much secrecy was not that the Russians would find out what HARP was about, but that some accounting office would."

"Yeah, but sooner or later we'd have to find out HARP I didn't work."

"Not if HARP II worked. Not if HARP III worked. What George Grove did was to figure out a way to make a ninety-percent profit on a weapons system. He got tired with thirty and forty percent. He got tired of selling shoddy rifles and non-spec weapons."

Remo saw the numbers move but he understood none of them.

"You see, what happened to Grove and, sadly, to some others who graduated from business schools was that they began to reduce the world to numbers. If you look at the numbers it makes sense to buy someone off rather than to build a product right. It's cheaper. We're getting away from that now, but there it is."

"Stealing is stealing. A pickpocket thinks the same way."

"You're right, of course," said Smith. "Unfortunately, a pickpocket has a lot better chance of getting caught. These numbers only confirm my suspicions. By the time these numbers might get to court, a lot of expensive accountants and lawyers will make them seem cleaner than the Better Business Bureau's books."

"But it's a fraud."

"Son, you blew the only hard evidence we had against him right out of court. Grove is probably filling his fire-insurance claim right now. I've got to hand it to our Mr. Grove. He is going to get richer and richer, safer and safer."

Remo couldn't believe what he was hearing.

"Grove is going to get his appropriations for a HARP II and a III and maybe even a IV. And no one is going to ask what happened to HARP I. It will end up just like the rest of that vast junkyard of obsolete weapons. Nobody cares whether they ever worked or not."

"And you think it's funny," said Remo. "Mac gives his life to get you that stuff so you can nail the bastard and now you're telling me he's going to get away with it, that we can't stop him?"

"You can," said Smith.

"For McCleary," said Remo. "I liked him."

"No," said Smith. "You are going to do it because it has to be done. There is no other way we can get at George Grove. It gives me a sense of pleasure that we are going to get someone who calculatedly is defecating on our country. But that pleasure is not what it is all about. That was not why McCleary gave his life. I knew that man longer than you did and I believe I felt closer to him than you could have. But McCleary does not matter, Remo."

"To you," said Remo.

Smith cleared his throat.

"You will eliminate George Grove with a natural kill. A perfect accident. I spoke to Chiun about that at the very beginning."

"Along with a few other things," said Remo.

"Well, you understand that was necessary," said Smith. "I hope. In any case, you can do the natural kill, can't you?"

"Sure, but it's not a natural kill. It only looks natural."

"Yes," said Smith. "That will do fine." He wondered how much Remo had really changed, as McCleary had warned. Already the young man was thinking differently. The New York City policeman they had kidnapped over a month before would have scarcely given a second thought to the difference between a kill appearing natural and being natural.

"Grove is at Mount Promise testing area. It may be one of the more heavily guarded sites in America. You will be going up against what is probably the technologically best protected site in the world. It has all the latest equipment, things that aren't even in production stage yet."

"What are you worried about?" asked Remo.

"I don't know how much of a chance you stand."

"Listen, half the new stuff you're talking about was probably forgotten a thousand years ago. I mean take HARP. Do you know the story of General Liu and the Emperor of the Shining Light? In the fifth dynasty, the generals were given the money to raise their own armies. General Liu had five armies defending the western provinces. But four of them were fake. He pocketed the rest of the money. Only one real army belonged to him and the emperor couldn't do anything against them."

"What happened?"

"The emperor hired Sinanju."

"And?"

"What do you mean 'and'? And he hired Sinanju."

"You mean Sinanju terminated the greedy general?"

"What do you think they did? Bring him to trial with evidence? They hung his head on a palace wall, gave half of his gold to the Master of Sinanju, put the emperor's brother in charge of the last remaining army, and gave laudations to Sinanju, as well as the added tribute. Sinanju."

"Do you want tribute, Remo?"

"I don't want anything from you, Smith. I don't need anything. What could I want? Hey, I'm the guy you got because nobody would miss him. Well, you chose right, you calculating lemon-faced . . . Good-bye."

"I'm sorry about the Chiun thing. Is that what's bothering you, Remo?" asked Smith. Remo was walking out of the main computer room.

"No. Nothing bothers me. That's the least of it. If I never see Chiun again, then good."

"It was just security, Remo."

"Right. You got the right man. I don't need anything. I don't want anything. I don't have anything. Or anyone."

And Remo left. Later, Smith requested the presence of the Master of Sinanju. Chiun listened in silence. There was a very dangerous place called Mount Promise. It was where America tested weapons. Remo was going to penetrate that place to remove an enemy. But it was a very dangerous place to penetrate. There were devices upon devices that would stop people from entering, things only the greatest minds could imagine.

Remo might not survive. He might become wounded. He might be captured. If that happened, Chiun was to fulfill the contract.

Chiun nodded.

"O gracious emperor, your commands are like the roaring thunder of the oncoming storm, unstoppable in their awesomeness. How well you fear for your subjects. You have feared so well that you have called upon Sinanju to enforce your will. We have had great success in the past with such defenses, and I am sure you will be pleased with Remo's services again."

It was almost a classic speech. What Chiun had said was the emperor should not insult Sinanju by suggesting there was something it could not do. Chiun could have told him five stories of such defenses, each one ending in a Sinanju victory. The only problem would be if Remo forgot his lessons like he did that day on the statue that so resembled the Korean cliffs. Then of course there could be problems.

"You won't have any problems executing Remo if you have to?" asked Smith. "I ask this because I think he has an emotional attachment to you. I think it bothered him when he found out you would have to kill him, under certain circumstances."

"Yes. I saw how it bothered him."

"You will not have any problems in this matter then?" asked Smith.

And Chiun answered in the room of the machines that Emperor Smith seemed to like so much:

"There is but one problem in the world, and that is that your glory is not fully recognized as yet."

"Well, all right," said Smith.

Chiun gave a proper retreating bow. He was rather pleased with his presentation before this mad devious white emperor who preferred machines to courtesans and silks. It never did an assassin any good to let an emperor really know what was on his mind. The one thing an emperor could not handle was the truth.

Even Remo had difficulty with it. It was an obsession with some whites. Fortunately not all. But they would dwell on the truth as though every passing leaf had to be informed of its greenness, every wart announced, every intention absolutely perfectly understood by anyone who happened past. Remo was like that. No matter what Chiun tried, that truthfulness seemed too stubbornly resistant to training, too immutable in the face of wisdom or logic.

Chiun thought about that as he packed for his passage to Mount Promise. He could not be blamed for that failure. After all, what could one do with the boy when the Roman Catholic Church had him for the first eighteen years of his life?

* * *

Mount Promise was a glorious piece of American scenery with high-rising peaks, magnificent natural pines, flowing streams, freshwater lakes, and machine-gun posts behind wire fences.

It was set in this isolated part of the American west to take advantage of its distance from everything. At Mount Promise, things could be blown up, shot up, lasered, strafed, tracked, and done in through mud, heat, rain, ice and other weather conditions of war without notice.

The combined powers at Mount Promise, it was said on this magnificent spring day, could track the thought of an ant at a mile, and incinerate it at twenty miles.

It was General Scott Watson who commented on the beauty of spring. It was George Grove who did not care that much about the spring day, but the testing of another of his weapons, the C-18.

General Watson offered to have George Grove personally delivered to the site so that he could oversee the test himself.

"I don't want to see it. Just make sure there are no screw-ups today, will you, Scott?"

General Watson, commander of the interoffice memo, conqueror of the congressional subcommittee, gave a snappy salute to a passing military guard as he guided George Grove to one of the administration buildings. He had a bit of bad news for Grove that day. It was nothing major, not like the sneak attack some foreign power had waged on HARP; just an update on the nuisance none of them had been able to get rid of.

Major Rayner Fleming would be on hand for the test of the C-18. Somehow, she had evaded enforced hospitalization. Worse yet, someone was condoning—if not encouraging—her special interest in anything Grove produced. But before the general got the chance to drop the bombshell on George Grove, the two men met her in an outer command room. Fleming was in uniform.

Grove squeezed General Watson's arm, indicating that he would take care of it. Grove understood women, especially this type. Women like Fleming had no desire to be men, as many suspected. What they wanted was control, acknowledgment that they ran things. Words never cost anyone anything, so George Grove told her how happy he was to see her. And he had a small confession to make.

"I feel I owe you an apology. I get pretty hot under the collar when people start telling me how to run my business. But I know you're just doing your job. And pretty darn well by the looks of it."

General Watson smiled in agreement. An officer who actually commanded men in combat had once told him that the way infantry would handle cavalry in the past was to let them through, dissipating the force of their charge. In other words, not confront an offensive move at the point of attack. This was what Grove was doing now. Maybe that was the right way to handle the major.

Grove exuded charm like a too-sweet car odorizer.

"Hell," said George Grove. "The important thing is we're both working for the same side, right?"

"Yes, Mr. Grove," said Major Fleming. "And speaking of work, I still have a lot to do before this afternoon . . ."

"Carry on, Major," said General Watson, happy that she was preparing to leave.

But Grove did not let it pass.

"Actually, General, there was one point I wanted

to clear up with the major," said Grove. He reached into his jacket pocket and produced several glossy photographs. He spread them on the table in front of Major Fleming.

"Who are you really working for?" he asked.

Major Fleming looked down at the photographs. There was that bird colonel from the auditor general's office in New York City, and that rather pushy companion she had on the elevator ride down. She wondered if she should tell. Then came another picture of the bird colonel, this time with his head on a pillow and tubes going into his nose.

"I'm sorry, Mr. Grove, but I have no idea what you're talking about."

General Watson looked to Grove. This he did not understand. He knew she probably was the leak to the news media, but this was more than Grove had yet to tell him.

"She's an informer. She's selling out the Army and betraying you, General Watson."

"George, I'm sure there's been some mistake," said General Watson.

"Shut up, Scott. These men are working for some secret government investigative unit and she is part of it."

Major Fleming did not miss the closeness apparent between the two men. She thought of Private D'Amico. Major Fleming was beginning to understand a lot more than she even suspected before.

"Where did you get those photographs?" she asked.

"That's none of your business," said Grove.

"If you will excuse me, General," she said to Watson, "I have other things to attend to."

"Who are you working for?" asked Grove.

"You are not my commanding officer, Mr. Grove. If you have an accusation I would appreciate your making a formal charge, and then backing it up. Now, I am busy," she said, picking up a folder on the specs of the C-18. She was going to make sure this weapon was perfect, down to every last screw and nut.

She was also going to see if someone could look into General Watson's finances. She smelled rotten apple. And she smelled it contaminating whatever part of the barrel it touched.

Remo gained entry to the Mount Promise compound rather easily. The flaw in a maximally defended castle was that the lords of that castle tended to believe no one could penetrate their beautiful defenses. But all defenses were designed only to protect against what most people could possibly do. They were not set to detect the presence of Sinanju, particularly when that presence came in on the underside of a speeding truck where normally there was no place for a person to hang on to.

Remo entered with the road an eighth of an inch from his cheek, going by at sixty miles an hour. When it slowed inside the compound, he allowed the momentum of the truck to roll him forward along the dust, careful not to muss his army slacks and private's blouse. He landed, of course, walking.

Major Rayner Fleming thought she must have failed to be aware of her surroundings because suddenly walking next to her was that wise guy from the elevator in New York City, the one whose picture she had just been shown by George Grove. Now he was dressed as an Army private.

"Some people are looking for you," she said.

"You remember me?" said Remo.

"How could I forget the longest elevator ride I have ever taken in my life? You've just gotten me into a pile of shit, you know. I'm supposed to be your accomplice in whatever it is you're up to. Now, who the hell are you, Private?"

"Would you believe the one loving human being in my entire organization?"

"You know, I could march you into that building," said Major Fleming, nodding to where she had just left General Watson and George Grove. "And that would clear up a lot of my problems right now."

"You could but you won't," said Remo. He laid on as much charm as his rough face could hold. Even that might not be enough, he thought. Maybe he'd give her a demonstration of Sinanju, treat her to the first of the thirty-seven steps, but that might leave her writhing in passion here on the test grounds. Worse, it might have no effect on her at all.

"Who the hell are you, giving me orders? Army Intelligence?"

Remo smiled. Stroking her cheek as one might stroke a lotus blossom seemed somewhat inappropriate at this point.

"You are Army Intelligence, aren't you?"

"You know I can't answer that," said Remo.

"You're up here on a case," she said.

Remo smiled.

"It's the AR-60, isn't it?"

Remo narrowed his eyes to look as though he knew what an AR-60 was. Maybe he could stroke her cheek as a lotus blossom after all of this was done.

"No wonder I've been having so much trouble getting information," said Major Fleming. "We've been working on the same thing. I'm sorry. I don't even know your name or rank. Do I salute you?"

Remo thought about that. What he thought was, Good-bye, lotus blossom. What he said was:

"You salute me."

Someone had been watching them, Remo knew. Major Fleming hadn't noticed, of course. He was well dressed, and he had been waiting for the proper moment, because just now he got into a jeep across the small dusty square and drove over to them. He seemed to recognize Major Fleming.

"Hello, my name is Wilson," he said. "I'm from Grove Industries, Major Fleming. General Watson asked me to contact you about an in-use weapon that has been fully tested already. The AR-60?"

"You're damned right I am concerned about the AR-60. Apparently someone doesn't realize that when an American soldier fires a rifle it is supposed to kill the other guy."

"I love it when you talk like George Patton," said Remo, who had seen a movie about the American general.

"I know you are not here for the AR-60 but I do have it set up in the C range, and I think you will like what you see. This time we are going to kill the other guy, so to speak. I guarantee it."

"I would appreciate that, Mr. Wilson," she said, getting into his jeep. "What are you waiting for, soldier?" she said to Remo. "A presidential invitation?"

There was something wrong here. There was something wrong with the way the man invited them, the way he sat, the smile. Everything was wrong. But Remo did not refuse the invitation.

He assumed he still had a duty to protect this woman. He could get Grove later.

The jeep drove to a pound cake of a building. No windows. One story. Flat. One door.

"We can use you, too, soldier," said Wilson.

He wanted Remo to follow. Remo listened to them talk about bayonet mounts, housings, and other mysterious terms of manufacture as he absorbed the essence of what was around him. The passageways were bare. The doors were not simple hinged things that swung, but massive sliding locking mechanisms. They passed a small-arms range. A black Labrador retriever growled at them.

"Hi," Remo said. "I met your cousin."

Major Fleming and Wilson argued about manufacture. Remo sensed there was a great deal of anger in Fleming about the gun. He saw the fine proportion of her backside underneath the army skirt. Chiun had not mentioned the proper strokes for that part of the body. Remo thought he could improvise if he had to.

Remo began to plan his improvisation in his mind as Wilson and Fleming continued their argument. They stood by a small cage, chest-high, mounted to the floor with bolts. Above them to the right was a glass window just underneath the ceiling. There were seats behind the window. Wilson said he would be right back. Only when the door shut behind him did Remo realize he had lost his concentration. He heard the slam of solid metal and the gasp of air power locks and ran to the door. It didn't open. And then Wilson appeared on the other side of the glass window. He had a friend with him now, a friend with a diamond tooth.

Then the gas started hissing up from the vents

in the floor. And Remo knew what the small cage was for. It held animals so people could see how quickly they died from the gas. They were in the testing chamber of a poison-gas facility.

The vents had valves. Remo got to them, and turned. The hissing stopped. Major Fleming staggered. Remo tried to wedge the glass out of the wall. He couldn't get an angle for the proper force. And he didn't know how to create force yet. That was supposed to come later.

Vents in the ceiling opened up. More gas. There would be no later. The diamond tooth was smiling. Wilson simply rubbed his hands as though a mess were at last being cleaned up.

Wilson left. Major Fleming was trying to breathe too hard. She was breathing too hard. She was going to kill herself on the gas. Remo got to her chest and pressed. Instinctively she moved her hands to protect her modesty. But Remo wanted something else. He wanted her to pass out, use less oxygen. Her panic was going to do her no good here. She couldn't run anywhere. Adrenaline would use up too much oxygen. He put her down as though she had fainted.

Stone saw the woman go down and then the man. The man dropped suddenly as though he didn't expect to succumb to the gas, and had somehow been caught by surprise. His tongue rolled out of his mouth, and his eyes went up into his forehead.

Stone put on the proper suit, removed the safety lock so it would look like an accident, and entered the gassing room.

Now that he had a hit, Stone intended to settle up for his misses. He allowed himself a delicious little kick into the man's groin. Unfortunately, the kick was stopped by closing thighs. Stone went forward.

He hardly felt the mask rip off his head. The rest of his body was in so much pain. He felt a vise at the back of his head, and his face was being rubbed into the glass. He couldn't stop this force. His face went round and round against the glass, and he heard the scream of scratching reverberate through his skull. The man was using Stone's diamond tooth to cut a hole in the glass. Stone knew it had worked when his head went through the hole.

Then he didn't know what else the man would do. It was hard to know things when someone else's two forefingers had entered your brain through the eyesockets.

With the glass weakened by a central hole, Remo shattered the rest of it, then pulled Major Fleming through.

And then he encountered the one great disadvantage of Sinanju. When one worked on a person's chest to restore breathing one did not employ the strokes to induce copulation for the purpose of reproduction.

Major Fleming apparently realized this also, because when she came to she thanked Remo, one officer to another.

George Grove heard about the death in the gas chamber over a light salad with a fine California dressing and a Greek wine in General Watson's private room. A captain interrupted. There had been an accident in the gas chamber. Grove was dining with both General Watson and his assistant, Wilson.

Wilson asked:

"What happened?"

He was happy to let the captain tell George Grove of his success.

"One of your assistants, Mr. Wilson, was killed in an accident in the gas chamber. A man named Stone, sir."

Wilson spilled the Greek wine on his paisley tie. The wine did not match.

As soon as Major Fleming's blouse was buttoned securely, Remo hustled her out of the building and due west, toward the woods. But Major Fleming was reluctant to go anywhere she would not find General Watson. She wanted the man arrested and she wanted to file a report right now.

"I'm not here for paperwork, Major. Come on. Don't slow up. It's good for your lungs."

"What are you going to do?"

"You don't have to know. And you don't want to know. I am going to take care of this thing. That's all."

"I want to report . . ."

"Sorry to pull rank on you, but we are going to do it my way. No red tape. No inquiries. Done nice and solid and final. How does that sound?"

"Sounds fine to me. Slow down. You run funny."

"I run funny? You're the one who can't keep up," said Remo. What was he supposed to do, pound his legs into the soil as though he were some form of ground basher?

"How do you run like that, that shuffle?"

"You just move. Move. Don't think. Move. Believe yourself, believe in yourself. Trust your essence."

"What?" said Major Fleming.

"Run like you always do—I'll wait."

But there was not much time for waiting. The

greatest advances in the technological age were about to be thrown at them on the proving grounds of Mount Promise.

General Scott Watson was going to direct this operation. It felt strange and exhilarating, commanding forces. It was pure soldiery.

Not that General Watson would want to do this for a living. "Gentlemen, I cannot overemphasize the importance of your task. Military secrets have been stolen and a man brutally slain. Major Fleming has been listed missing."

"How did they get in? What are they doing?" asked a major. "This post has never been penetrated."

"It may be part of an overall attack on our research capabilities. We have suffered losses already in a West Virginia site. Some of you may know about it."

"The same ones are here now?"

"We think so," said General Watson. "And that is the luckiest thing that ever could have happened to us. We have located them, we have bracketed them. Heat sensors have picked them up running within the perimeter of the camp."

A defense contractor many of the officers recognized stood beside General Watson. He was George Grove. He nodded agreement with the general.

"You must apprehend them now. You cannot let them get away. You have the equipment and with it you have an overwhelming advantage. There is no excuse for not getting them," said General Watson.

"If there is resistance, can we return fire, sir?" This from a captain.

General Watson hesitated. He was cool enough

not to show his surprise when George Grove spoke for him.

"The security of the United States is at risk, soldier. What do you think?" asked Grove. The young officers rushed to their equipment. It was a grand opportunity to practice on live targets.

But Remo's concern was not new technology as he moved through the woods. Something deadlier than a computer chip was in the woods.

He kept Major Fleming from stumbling as they moved down the mountainside. He spotted some edible berries as they ran. They were not as perfect as rice but he had not eaten that day. Major Fleming didn't want any berries. She just wanted to keep her balance. She told him her first name. It was Rayner.

The berries were good.

"Haven't eaten this good for weeks," said Remo.

Rayner Fleming ran with her legs breaking the downward run. Remo told her to allow her body to move, not to worry about the legs. She tried it. She fell into his arms. The legs had gone. Funny, it seemed so easy to Remo.

"Better use your legs to run," said Remo. "Do what you can. We should hit the lake and the road pretty soon, then we can get you . . ."

Remo halted. He listened. Rayner Fleming heard nothing. But then her lungs were gasping for air so hard that she couldn't hear anything but her breath. But this man knew something was around. He signaled for her to remain still, and then with the silent move of a cat, feet like slow, careful paws, Remo moved toward a large pine tree. He began to circle it. Rayner saw him move a hand forward as if to touch something on the far side of the tree. Suddenly Remo was in the air, flying up twice the height of a man and then landing on his back.

He had been thrown in such a way that he lost his center. Only one man knew that it was just the thing he needed to land on his feet. And only one man could have done that to him.

A delicate oriental figure came from behind the pine. It was Chiun. Remo knew the Master of Sinanju had come to kill him.

15

"Are you deaf?" asked Chiun. "I have been stomping around for ten minutes while you talk nonsense with this woman."

"It's a pleasure to meet you, too," said Major Fleming.

"Even worse," said Chiun, ignoring her. "You and this woman gorged yourself on sweets."

"Excuse me, but I do have a name," said Rayner Fleming.

"Women should make babies, not talk," said Chiun, still angered at the clumsy way Remo had moved through the forest. He had never taught him to move that way. Who had taught him to move that way?

Rayner Fleming had never been treated like this.

"I see you two went to the same charm school," she said.

"He always talks like that," said Remo. "He's Korean."

"I see. And I suppose that explains why he lives in a forest," she said.

"Actually, he came here for a special purpose. To kill me," said Remo.

"Kill you?" said Chiun. "You kill yourself. You eat sweets while you run. You take up with women for their looks. I do not have to kill you."

"Then why did you come?" said Remo.

"I am here to see that you do not bring shame to the House of Sinanju."

"And if I do, you'll kill me," said Remo.

What could Chiun say? That Remo was too good to be allowed to die just for a single emperor? After all, the world was full of kings and presidents and tyrants, but at most, there were only two real assassins alive at the same time. Chiun had already put in a lot of work. Where would he get another Remo?

This of course could not be uttered. Who knew what Remo would tell the devious and cunning Smith? Whites were too free with the truth and the truth was the last thing one told an emperor under any circumstances. So Chiun could not yet trust Remo with the fact that he would never kill him for a mere leader. No matter how his feelings were hurt.

"Yes, I would kill you," said Chiun. "Reluctantly, of course, because you have been a good pupil . . . for a white man."

"Oh, I see. Well, don't think that makes everything okay," said Remo. "Because it doesn't. Not here. Not with me."

"You're skinny," Chiun said to Rayner Fleming. If Remo were going to breed, he should have considered correct womb size.

"You're not square with me," said Remo, getting up from the ground.

"You're mad," said Chiun. "How typical. You don't ask me who you should breed with, or whether you should reproduce at this time, or whether there is a nice Korean girl available to you from a family we know something about. You dwell on your own private little injustice."

Chiun waved a hand. He didn't want to hear any more about it. He had already heard once today that Remo was unhappy about the possibility of Chiun killing him, and he didn't want to hear it again. There were things to do. Properly.

All three moved down the mountain, Remo staying close to Rayner, Chiun making sure Remo's hands helping her were being used for balance only.

Rayner didn't even see it until it was too late, until actually she was safe. She was busy trying to keep up when suddenly there was a clanging scream of metal, and a giant bear trap closed beneath her knee. But there was no pain. Was that the first numb reaction? She saw her leg behind her, the heel up. Her knee hurt. But it was because Remo was holding it firmly behind her. The bear trap had closed on a log and she hadn't even seen Remo's hand move.

"Correct," said Chiun.

"That was fantastic," said Rayner. "Who are you guys?"

"Fantastic is not another word for correct," said Chiun. "Remo, you must stop hanging around with your own kind."

Rayner noticed that Remo seemed pleased with the old man's simple comment, "correct." Were they crazy?

Just beyond one of the test ranges, they saw a logging truck. Chiun turned to Remo.

"She doesn't run well," he said with a nod toward the major. "We'll have to drive her."

"I qualified for my physical," snapped Rayner Fleming. "I passed every obstacle course."

"For whom?"

"For the Green Berets, the toughest fighting men in the world," said Rayner.

"They're soldiers, about twice as good as the average soldier," Remo explained to Chiun as they helped Rayner run. "Twice as tough. Twice as smart. Twice as well-conditioned."

"Twice?" asked Chiun.

"Right," said Remo. "I'll get the truck."

A logger was on his back trying to fix it when he saw the whole caboodle take off above his head down the road. Remo kept his foot on the floor. Chiun watched from the passenger's side, curious at how these machines moved. Rayner sat between them waiting for the whole rig to go crashing off the side of the road. Remo drove like a madman.

He drove them right toward a logging conveyor, right toward the logs.

His solution for that was jumping for their lives.

He made it, taking Rayner with him. Chiun, however, went down with the cab of the truck. It crushed trees underneath like twigs as it gathered momentum down the mountainside, spinning like a toy but landing, finally, like a truck, on its side, with a heavy crash.

Remo called down to the twisted metal and smoke, "You okay?"

There was no answer. He put Rayner Fleming down so that she could stand, and ran down to the truck.

"Oh, God. Chiun. Chiun. Are you okay?" yelled Remo.

Slowly, a twisted door moved, and Chiun

emerged, somewhat shaken, a door handle in his palm.

"Chiun, are you all right?"

"In Korea, door handles do not break," said Chiun.

"Are you hurt?"

"No. Of course not, my son," said Chiun.

"What did you call me?" asked Remo. He heard the words. He had been called a son by the Master of Sinanju.

"I called you a clumsy oaf. You drive like a monkey in heat."

But Remo had heard the right words first. Chiun could not erase them. The world was good. The sun was above them, and all the trees and water of the lakes were in their gloriously right places. Remo threw back his head and laughed. He would have hugged Chiun, but he doubted he could get a grip on him.

"You have a job to finish," snapped Chiun.

"I'll leave you the girl, the skinny one," said Remo.

"What are we going to do now?" asked Rayner.

"You're going to stay with Chiun. He'll probably teach you to breathe. I have a job to finish."

"I am not skinny," said Rayner Fleming.

"Don't embarrass us," said Chiun.

"I won't, little father," said Remo.

Rayner Fleming saw only a few fast movements before Remo disappeared into the trees. The oriental called Chiun was still watching him. There was a sense of pleasure on his face. She had seen that before, that joyous inner pleasure of mothers outside schoolyards watching their children learn to play for themselves.

* * *

The command center had the target triangulated. They notified General Watson in his staff car.

Grove and Wilson were with him.

"They have triangulation on him," said Grove.

Wilson nodded. A vast array of weaponry was trained on the target even though that target was within Mount Promise's own technological sites. But their nuisance was a dead man. That was guaranteed. All General Watson had to do now was say fire. But General Watson hesitated.

George Grove explained almost with the tiredness of talking to a not-too-alert child:

"Scott, it's your ass, too. We go. You go. Jail, Scott, can be a real career problem."

"Swat him," said General Watson.

"Good for you, Scott," said George Grove.

Remo was alone in the woods when the first ugly whine of a devastator shell reverberated through the forest. Remo did not know what the shell could do. But he knew where it was going to land, and that spot was very close to him.

There were no caves or rocks to hide behind. A blanket of shrapnel could not be dodged. Even worse, shells landing in woods made the very trees into pieces of shrapnel. There was nothing on this desolate piece of ground but Remo and an anthill and neither of them had much prospect of making it to the next second.

But an anthill meant earth. They didn't build in rock. Remo gathered himself, took two smooth steps, and moved down into the mound, deep into the darkness of the earth, as though it were sand, as though this were training, as though his only purpose in life was correct. The earth was dark and rich to the senses, and when the shell landed, it was as though someone had jumped on him while he was curled under a blanket.

Above ground the devastator cleared the trees, cleared the grass and removed the anthill. It had made Mother Nature ready for a parking lot. All one needed was the asphalt.

Command center registered the perfect hit. They also registered something else, something one of the officers said had to be impossible, but it had to be reported to General Wason anyhow.

"Target hit, sir, and target resumes locomotion, sir. Target proceeding to red four. Red four, sir."

Watson, Grove, and Wilson were quiet. Grove inhaled deeply. Wilson cleaned an imaginary speck off his perfect lapel. The devastator had hit and somehow missed. The target was still moving.

Remo brushed the dirt off him as he ran on the surface. The strange thing about the earth was how incredibly fresh it smelled underneath, as though it was rich with air when, of course, there wasn't enough air to breathe.

He did not know he was in target area red four or that this time an entire pattern was going to be used on him, and the pattern was in his last hiding place. He was running through a minefield and he discovered it as the charges started to go off, turning trees into shards of rockets, burning the grass, making pebbles into bullets whizzing by his head.

The earth had been turned against him but Remo ran ahead of it, and from it, right to the edge of a gully and into space. Where and how he would land he would figure out when he got there.

He fell. He did not judge the fall by height, but it was too high. The landing was hard, even in the trees. He went down, snapping branches, until the last one creaked and caught him. He felt his bones. All there. But there was blood on his hands. He had been cut.

And the tree was moving. It was moving upward. It wasn't a tree, it was a log. Other logs were moving upward. They were all moving under a long cable, over a deeper gorge.

Remo looked up. Behind him there were logs bobbing and dancing along this metal line. It was an eagle cable. He had read about them once when he was a youngster. They were used for clearing whole forests, a movable assembly line that took trees from where they were cut and ran them to where they could be finished.

Unfortunately they were not designed for passengers. Remo struggled up the breaking branches, trying to get to the top of the log.

He saw a good place to jump but that good place vanished as the logs moved downward. And beneath him was a deep canyon. Heights again.

Grove, Wilson and Watson heard the army track the target. It had escaped again.

"What is the matter? I am not asking you to commit genocide. Kill one man, for heaven's sake," said Grove.

"He's heading for the lake," said General Watson. "He's outside the compound in a logging operation. He's riding a log. We're near there."

"Then let's go. This should not be that hard, Scott," said Grove. He looked to Wilson, shaking his head. "The man is on a log. Logs are not the fastest, most elusive target in the world, General."

"Right," said General Watson. He nodded to his driver to step on it. The car pulled away with such speed that the armed soldier next to the driver almost fell out.

They arrived at the line of logs with plenty of time for the armed soldier to steady his rifle and aim, then wait for the right log to come down. The one with the man clinging to it.

It was like a shooting gallery, with one exception. When the soldier saw the man clinging to the log, he thought it seemed more like murder than target practice. He hesitated.

The important manufacturer grabbed the rifle himself, commenting acidly about the quality of the modern American soldier. He fired as the log went by, and missed the man who kept himself on its opposite side, much the same way American Plains Indians rode with their bodies hidden by the horse itself.

But Grove knew men, and Wilson had smelled the final blood. Wilson himself got behind the wheel of the car, and Grove joined him, cradling the rifle in his lap. General Watson, as he had been all along, was just along for the ride, going where Grove and Wilson decided to take him. They were going to finish what General Watson had failed to do.

They arrived where the cable let go of the logs, almost getting hit themselves. One log dropped. Then another. And another. Finally Grove saw him. He unloaded an entire clip into the log, watching chips fly, watching the man crawl like a bug, then he unloaded another clip.

General Watson warned him about the falling logs.

Grove continued to fire. Kill the bug, he thought. Kill the bug.

He thought he had him when the first log crashed into the command car. Remo heard the last bullet whistle by his head, and then looked down. It was safe to jump.

He heard the car crash above him on the mountain, heard the logs roll into steel siding. They were there. The man who had been firing at him was George Grove. Remo moved toward the car. Bodies had been thrown out. A general and a well-dressed civilian lay in that putty-strange way of dead bodies. Grove might be already dead.

And then Remo made a mistake. He had allowed his mind to think too much, and he had shut off his senses. They came back only when he heard the voice.

"Okay, that's far enough."

Remo looked above him. There was George Grove with a service revolver.

"I used to be interested in who you worked for. Now I don't give a shit."

Grove stepped closer. He felt the strong blood joy of death. And then, of course, the irony of it all.

"You know, they are going to give me a medal for killing you. I am saving America from a saboteur."

And for the sheer pleasure of it, he decided to shoot off the testicles first.

He fired twice. The man jerked twice. But the man was still there. More important, the two bullets hadn't even unzipped his fly.

And the man was closing on him. George Grove was a marksman. He didn't miss. He aimed two more bullets right into the man's chest, only to penetrate the trees behind the chest.

He fired again, and the man came closer. And then the target had the gun and was casually dispensing the last bullet harmlessly on the ground.

"Who are you?"

Remo would have answered George Grove, but

he was busy. There was work to do. George Grove felt himself lifted to the overturned command car. He could have sworn this man was whistling a tune from a children's movie. A pleasant joyful little tune that had been sung by the dwarfs in *Snow White*. It was "Whistle While You Work."

The man held George Grove like a basket of goodies. Grove could not move. He felt the man bend down. He saw the man gather two twigs in one hand. He saw the twigs turn in that hand, turn so fast they began to smoke, and then, with a puff, there was a flame.

Remo put George Grove into the back seat of the command car, broke his kneecaps with two quick taps of a finger and then touched the burning twigs to the gasoline that had spilled from the tank.

George Grove went up like a marshmallow.

It was not, of course, an accidental death. But it would look like an accident. It would be good enough for Smith.

Rayner Fleming was waiting at lakeside, but Chiun was not there.

"He went to look for you, Remo," she said.

"I didn't need him. I did it. I didn't need him," said Remo. He jumped into a speedboat tied to the dock. "Now I have to look for him. I didn't need him at all and now he's gone."

Then they saw Chiun, saw him almost at the same time as they saw the soldiers, truckloads of them, disgorging onto the jetty, coming between them and Chiun.

"He blew it, not me," said Remo. The soldiers aimed their rifles, and then they all saw it. No one missed it, especially not Remo, whose mouth fell open for a moment.

Chiun, Master of Sinanju, raised up his chin and, with delicate precision, ran, his sandals moving with the lightness of eagle down, across the shortest distance from shore to jetty, not even making a single splash on the waves.

The soldiers kept their aim, but the fingers froze on the triggers. A man was running across the water.

No one fired at Chiun, and then the frail figure was in the speedboat, and the two of them took off in a plume of white spray.

Major Rayner Fleming signaled all riflemen to stand down.

"Who the hell are they?" asked an officer running up to the end of the jetty.

"Would you believe, the good guys," said Major Fleming.

Chiun, delighted to see Remo successful and whole, examined his pupil. Remo was satisfied with himself.

"Correct?" he asked Chiun.

"The great assassins never appeared to try that hard," Chiun said. "And you are cut."

"The target is dead and I am alive," said Remo. "It is correct. There is no almost correct."

"Well," said Chiun, "if showing that you could almost be killed is good enough for you . . ." His voice trailed off, his shoulders moved in a questioning shrug, and his long fingernails fluttered briefly like a dove alighting comfortably on a branch.

"Correct is enough for me, little father," said Remo. He was angry. He never thought he would ever meet anyone who could take the bloom off getting out alive.

ABOUT THE AUTHORS

WARREN MURPHY has written eighty books in the last twelve years. His novel *Trace* was nominated for the best book of the year by The Mystery Writers of America and twice for best book by The Private Eye Writers of America. *Grand Master*, co-written with his wife Molly Cochran, won the 1984 Edgar Award. He is a native and resident of New Jersey.

RICHARD SAPIR is a novelist with several book club selections. He is a graduate of Columbia University and lives with his wife in New Hampshire.

CHRISTOPHER WOOD is a novelist with over fifty books in print, and has written two James Bond screenplays in addition to the screenplay for Remo. He was born and raised in London.